THE BYZANTIUM B...

'Bridie wondered what would ha...
*Dear Aunt Dolly . . . Gramps a...
am living with complete strangers i...
spend most evenings with tramps .*

Bridie's grandfather has vanished, a... ...acing
Crickbone brothers have taken over his yard. Suddenly
Bridie finds herself all alone in the city. It never looked so
strange and threatening before. But then she begins to
discover friends in the unlikeliest of places, and ends up
meeting Miss Firbanks, owner of the Byzantium Bazaar, a
department store where time stands still and dust covers
everything.

Now all Bridie has to do is solve the mystery of what
happened to Gramps, and for that she enlists the help of the
street people.

Don't expect Aunt Dolly to approve . . .

Stephen Elboz lives in Northamptonshire. He has done a
variety of jobs, including being a dustman, a civil servant,
and a volunteer on an archaeological dig. He is now a
teacher, and writes in his spare time.

ALSO BY STEPHEN ELBOZ:

The House of Rats
Winner of the 1992 Smarties Young Judges Prize for the 9–11
age category.

'A brilliant story which grips you from the first to last page.'
The Mail on Sunday

THE BYZANTIUM BAZAAR

Other books by Stephen Elboz

The House of Rats
The Games-Board Map
Bottle Boy

THE
BYZANTIUM
BAZAAR

Stephen Elboz

Oxford University Press
Oxford New York Toronto

DAMAGED

For Brian Winkworth and Jayne Redding
(remembering our times together at the O.T.).

Oxford University Press, Walton Street, Oxford OX2 6DP

Oxford New York
Athens Auckland Bangkok Bombay
Calcutta Cape Town Dar es Salaam Delhi
Florence Hong Kong Istanbul Karachi
Kuala Lumpur Madras Madrid Melbourne
Mexico City Nairobi Paris Singapore
Taipei Tokyo Toronto

and associated companies in
Berlin Ibadan

Oxford is a trade mark of Oxford University Press

Copyright © Stephen Elboz 1996
First published 1996

Cover design: Slatter-Anderson
Cover illustration: Bob Harvey

A CIP catalogue record for this book is available
from the British Library

ISBN 0 19 271578 X

Printed and bound in Great Britain by
Biddles Ltd, Guildford and King's Lynn

CHAPTER ONE

CITIES HAVE THEIR own kinds of stars, Bridie decided, a mixture of satellites and winking space junk and slowly moving jets too high up to hear.

Weary of tugging her suitcase, she stopped and perched herself on it, briefly surveying the clear February sky.

Then she blinked and gazed about her.

The narrow, rutted street was deserted and poorly lit. It smelt of oil and unemptied dustbins; and its factories and warehouses leant towards her as if eavesdropping. On a patch of ground on the corner, shadowy lorries congregated like a herd of grazing dinosaurs. And distantly the moon was appearing from behind some high-rise offices, their lights ablaze and honeydew yellow, except for the few that were turned out, leaving gaps like the gaps in a perfect smile.

The girl sighed. 'Mustn't sit here wasting any more time,' she told herself. 'Especially when I'm still not sure if this is the right way.'

Of course, Aunt Dolly would have been horrified; so horrified in fact that she would have taken a pen and dashed down her reasons in a list which might have gone something like this:

A. Bridie was on her own.

B. Bridie was in that particular part of the city at that particular time.

C. Her careful arrangements to have Bridie met at the bus station had been disregarded.

D. You can't trust anyone to do anything properly these days.

E. Bridie had, at that very moment, wiped her nose on

her scarf (and wasn't there a perfectly good clean handkerchief in her pocket?).

F. There was so much in the world to disapprove of and be horrified by.

G. . . . Well, *G* didn't matter any more. Suddenly Bridie let out a cry of delight and thoughts of Aunt Dolly vanished like vapour. Ahead, the girl had caught sight of a familiar landmark. It was the Devil.

Not the real Devil of course, but a Devil on a billboard, higher than the roof-tops. Above him, fiery letters spelt out *Poona Curry Paste. Devilishly Hot. Devilishly Good.* Eagerly Bridie watched him, anticipating his one special trick. Then mysteriously the Devil's lips parted and out slipped a smoke ring, uncoiling in the breeze.

Bridie laughed delightedly as if at a favourite uncle performing his Christmas party piece. 'Hello, Devil!' she called lugging her case towards him.

By recognizing the billboard the rest of the dark street became familiar too. Bridie knew that her Devil stood on the corner of Rivet Lane and Mandrel Street, next to the scrapyard; and at the end of the lane was her grandfather's home and business.

Really it was no more than a neat little house surrounded by a yard. Nothing grew in the yard, but set out as pleasingly as flower beds, or as regular as vegetable plots, were the rows of cast-iron fireplaces, pine doors, stained-glass panels, fancy railings, columns, chimney pots, and window frames—along with many other items rescued from old buildings that were being pulled down and which might be re-used again. They were like pieces of a gigantic jigsaw puzzle, but all methodically ordered.

Although she approved of order, Aunt Dolly didn't approve of Gramps's business. It was too dusty and dirty; and why couldn't folk buy new things if they wanted them? To her mind the yard wasn't the magical place it was to Bridie and her grandfather, full of different possibilities.

Aunt Dolly saw only junk and worthless bric-à-brac.

Turning down Rivet Lane, Bridie passed the high corrugated fence of the neighbouring scrapyard. Dimly, just on the bend, she could see the double gates of Gramps's yard—and the wonderful names of the old chimney pots came flooding back to her. *The imperial flute, the crested windsor, the salt-glazed castle, the coved wind foil.* All like chessmen and standing as tall as a young child. She began to hurry, dragging her squeaking case behind her.

And then she stopped, the suitcase butting the backs of her legs.

Gramps's name and trade—Samuel Summers: Architectural Salvager—remained elegantly scrolled across the gates, but underneath in paint-dripped letters was scrawled:

No hawkers

No circulars

No busybodies

Nobody!

And over the top was an ugly tangle of new barbed wire.

Puzzled, Bridie pushed at the gates. They opened an inch before a chain prevented them from going further. Strange, Gramps never usually locked up until he went to bed.

She stepped back into the road.

'Gramps!'

She waited.

'Gramps, are you there? It's me, Gramps, it's . . . '

Her voice trailed off into silence. Someone was watching her through a spyhole.

'Gramps?' whispered Bridie. 'Is that you?'

A brief silence followed, then a hoarse voice whispered, 'Go away!'

Bridie took a step closer. 'You're not Gramps!' she said fiercely.

She heard a second voice behind the gate hiss, 'Who is it?'

'Some girl,' said the first voice.

'Some girl?'

'Some girl.'

'What does it want?' demanded the second voice.

'I don't know.'

'Ask it—ask it!'

The eye refocused on Bridie.

'What do you want?'

'Mr Summers—my grandfather. He lives here. You better open up and let me in.'

The spyhole slammed shut. Bridie heard urgent whispers on the far side.

'You said . . . '

'I said . . . ?'

'But . . . '

'Say nothing . . . '

'Nothing?'

'Nothing.'

A moment later Bridie heard the rattle of chains and the gate creaked open just enough to reveal two of the most peculiar creatures she had ever seen. Stooped and crooked, wrong-boned and brittle—they resembled those thousand-year-old leather men occasionally dug up in bogs or left unfrozen when ice retreats up a mountain; and it was more fitting to ask *what* they were, before considering *who* they might be.

Nor were their looks the most peculiar thing about them. Nor again was it because they were twins—identical down to the very last squint, sneer, and cock of an eyebrow. It was because in every action they were so precisely alike that the effect was quite disconcerting. They blinked at the same time, turned at the same time, and sometimes spoke their words at the same time. And if one did not follow the other as closely as a mirror image, he was bound to do so a few seconds later.

Instinctively Bridie drew back.

'Where is my grandfather?' she demanded.

The brothers looked at her, then slyly at each other, and back at the girl again. Their mouths were so crooked it was impossible to tell if they were smiling mockingly or frowning with contempt.

'There is no other soul here . . . '

'. . . but us,' began the first brother and finished the second. They drew closely together as if they might merge and become one.

'But this is my grandfather's yard,' cried Bridie. 'See, that's his name on the gates: Mr Samuel Summers.'

'Ahum!' One brother cleared his throat, the other did likewise.

'He had to . . . '

'Had to go away . . . '

'Leave.'

'Urgently.'

'Packed his case.'

'And went.'

'Family business.'

'No forwarding address.'

'No time to write it down.'

'No nothing.'

'Just gone.'

Bridie could feel tears of frustration pricking her eyes. 'But . . . but . . . the only family he has is me and Aunt Dolly and he wouldn't just leave without telling us where he was going. Didn't he get Aunt Dolly's letter?'

'No letters here.'

'Only us.'

'We get no letters.'

'Nailed up the letter box.'

'And if we did we wouldn't open them.'

'Not addressed to us, see.'

'We're not Samuel Summers.'

'We're Amos . . . '

'. . . and Deakin Crickbone.'

They grinned.

'We're the caretakers.'

Now Bridie stared at the brothers with deepest suspicion, realizing they were wearing her grandfather's clothes.

Sleeves and trousers rode up ridiculously short on them; and although dressed in Mr Summers's Sunday-best suits, they had swapped jackets in an effort to look as similar to each other as possible through the resulting mismatch of check and herringbone.

Cuffs and collars were greasy, food stained the fine hand-stitched waistcoats; buttons were missing and knees worn.

If anything, Mr Summers was a dapper man. He wore a carnation in his buttonhole and a bowler hat, even when clambering amongst dusty rubble. Now the Crickbones wore his hats—riding too small on their heads, both crowns punched through like lids.

The sight proved too much for Bridie. Giving an angry shout, she pushed forwards, threatening to snap the brittle stick insects if they got in her way, and dragging her squeaking suitcase behind like some poor creature on its way to market. Hardly had she gone a dozen steps before she stopped, gazing around in horror.

The neat rows of rare and wonderful pieces rescued from derelict buildings were no longer there. Everything had been swept back to the fence and heaped up without care. Chimney pots were broken and stained glass smashed; while the charred frames of old pine doors remained clearly visible in the cold ash of a dead fire. Standing in the middle of its patch of naked ground, Gramps's house looked as forlorn and neglected as the rest of the yard.

As Bridie stood staring in disbelief, bony fingers coiled around her arms like tendrils. She looked up to see an identical expression upon either side, smiling nastily.

'But Gramps would never have allowed you to do this to

his yard,' she protested weakly. 'And where are his animals?'

'Animals?'

Amos and Deakin caught each other's eye. With a touch of menace they said, 'What do you know about *animals*?'

Bridie stared at them, not understanding the meaning of this darker tone. She felt their grip tighten.

'Gramps had a donkey called Trotter,' she explained. 'It used to pull his cart. Gramps didn't like lorries. Thought them too noisy and smelly.'

'No donkey here,' said Amos dismissively.

Bridie sprang back at once. 'What about his cats? Gramps loved his cats.'

'Cats!' Both brothers spat the word contemptuously.

'Definitely no cats,' said Amos.

'Hate cats, we do,' said Deakin.

'Nasty, vicious, wicked things.'

'Mean, biting, scheming brutes.'

'But they kept the mice down and Gramps said—'

'We told you,' snarled the brothers together. 'No cats!'

'Then what about Gramps's chickens?'

Bridie felt a jolt go through the Crickbones like electricity. Fingers bit into her arm making her squirm.

'Ow—you're hurting me!' she cried.

'Chickens?' breathed Deakin. 'What do you know about chickens, girl?'

'Only that Gramps kept them behind the house for their eggs. It was the only way he was sure they were fresh and—'

'Well, there ain't no chickens left neither,' snarled both brothers.

'You start spreading it round we got chickens and we'll have the law on you.'

'Nasty little troublemaker.'

'Coming here with these cock-and-bull stories of yours.'

'Then accusing us of keeping chickens.'

'Wicked rumour monger.'

Bridie found herself being prodded back towards the open gates.

'But . . . but . . . you can't send me away,' she cried. 'Where can I go? And what about Gramps? You still haven't told me where Gramps has gone.'

The Crickbones gave her one final push, sending her sprawling across the pavement. The gates slammed and the chains rattled.

Immediately Bridie flew back, hammering upon the gates with her fists.

'Hey!' she shouted. 'You've got my case in there! Give me back my case!'

She banged and called until she knew it was useless, and falling against the gates burst into tears.

'Oh!'

She stopped crying as abruptly as she had started.

Someone was standing in the darkened roadway—standing and watching her with rapt curiosity.

Chapter Two

Seeing herself discovered, the little figure turned and scuttled away. It was obvious she was not accustomed to doing anything involving a degree of speed, for upon her back was a large cardboard box which, besides containing everything in the world she owned, made her resemble a human snail and, as it so happened, also gave rise to her nickname. The pans attached to her coat tail clanked and rattled. In hobbling to get away, she made more noise than a one-man band.

'Wait!' called Bridie running after her. 'Oh, please wait!'

Snail wore a balaclava with an old battered hat on top. Her head was bowed beneath the weight of her load. When Bridie caught her up, she glared suspiciously at the girl, a drip quivering on the end of her nose.

'Ain't seen nuffin'. Don't know nuffin'. Don't bovver no one,' she said in one breathless wheeze.

'But I haven't *asked* you anything yet,' said Bridie.

'Don't matter none,' muttered Snail. 'Same rule applies. Godda keep yer nose clean.' As if to demonstrate she sniffed long and hard, making the drip dance but not entirely disappear.

She turned to go, the pans clanking. Hurriedly Bridie said, 'I'm looking for my grandfather—Samuel Summers—he used to live over there. Smart man in a bowler hat. You would have known him for sure if you come from these parts. Everyone knew Gramps.'

The head slowly turned back to regard her. 'Can't says I don't—can't says I do,' said Snail infuriatingly.

'*Won't* you mean,' cried Bridie suddenly losing her

temper and then just as quickly regretting it. 'Ple-ase, I don't want much—'

'You best ask someone else, I 'as work t'do.'

The pans swung back into life as she went on her way. With nowhere else to go and a little curious as to what this work might be, Bridie found herself trotting after the old woman.

They hadn't gone far before Snail stopped by a hole in the road, tilting her head in contemplation. To Bridie it appeared just an ordinary hole—and a common enough nuisance along any street. Around it yellow warning lights blinked, while dimly, at the bottom, earthenware pipes gleamed.

Snail scratched her chin and taking extreme care edged her way around the hole, minutely studying it from every possible angle. Yet it wasn't until after a few minutes of careful watching that Bridie realized the actual hole was of no importance to Snail and the true objects of her interest were the cones surrounding it.

'What are you doing?' asked Bridie.

'Shhhh!'

Snail stood in front of each cone in turn muttering, 'Ain't you . . . Ain't you . . . Ain't you . . . '

Then she made a decision. 'This is the one!' she declared triumphantly, and pouncing on a cone that appeared neither more nor less different from all the others, made off with it, laboriously counting her steps until she reached her twenty-third when, pointlessly, she set it down in the middle of the pavement.

Bridie remained puzzled. She understood Snail's actions no better for having seen them. A sort of game sprang to mind, in which the cones were movable pieces like pawns in chess. Unbending her back as much as the box would allow, Snail looked mighty pleased with herself. She shook the dew-drop with a sniff.

'Must get on,' she said. 'The 'lectricity board 'as the road up in Granville Street. Them cones there are red and white. Worth double points.'

She began hobbling away.

'Who . . . who do you play against?' ventured Bridie.

Snail stopped but did not turn around. 'The city, of course,' she muttered after a moment's silence.

'So it *is* a game!' cried Bridie, pleased with herself. 'And are there rules and forfeits like in other games?'

'Might be,' said Snail guardedly.

'Can I play?'

'No!' Snail's reply was as swift as a bite. 'Can't. Against the rules, see. Just me and the city. We've been playin' each uver f'years and years.'

'So when will your game finish?' asked Bridie.

Snail smiled. 'When I dies and am in my grave.' She wheezed a kind of grim laughter. 'I'll make do with a cone for me 'eadstone.'

This struck Bridie as unfair. 'But that means the city will win in the end.'

She heard Snail softly chuckle. ''Course not,' said the old woman. '*I* shall win because the city'll 'ave no one left to play against.'

Her pans swayed and clanked—but only for a few paces. Then she stopped as if frozen by a sudden thought.

'Samuel Summers?' Bridie heard her mutter.

'Yes—yes,' cried the girl eagerly, running up to her. 'So you *do* know something after all—maybe even where he is?'

Defensively Snail rucked up her shoulders. 'Ain't seen nuffin'. Don't know nuffin'. Don't bovver no one . . . But Mr Summers, 'im a good sort. Gave me m'pans 'e did. No holes in 'em niver.' She sniffed. 'Best go back where you comes from, girl.'

Bridie's voice broke with a sob. 'I can't!'

Snail was silent for a long time. Bridie wondered if she had fallen asleep. Some folk can do that—fall asleep on their feet. But then she turned her head abruptly, making Bridie start.

'You 'ungry?'

'Yes . . . I suppose . . . ' said Bridie. 'But the Crickbones have my money. Everything I had was in my suitcase.'

'You know Soap Hill?'

Bridie nodded. 'With the old soap factory on top? Yes, I know it.'

'Go there,' advised Snail. 'Good people there—they'll give you grub. Wiv some'in' in your belly you'll think straight.'

This said, Snail hobbled away into the darkness gleefully muttering, 'Double points for red and white . . . big score waitin' in Granville Street . . . '

CHAPTER THREE

WITH ONE FINAL, hopeless glance back at Gramps's yard, Bridie set off for Soap Hill. She had no idea what she would find there, but was glad to be clear of Rivet Lane and the Crickbones. Retracing her steps quickly brought her back to the curry-paste Devil. He grinned, blowing out a mocking smoke ring at her.

In no mood to be teased, Bridie crossed the iron canal bridge to Soap Hill.

Once there had been streets of houses on Soap Hill, homes for the factory workers, with names like Bubble Crescent, Foam Heights, and Lather View. But when the soap factory closed the community gradually drifted away. Street after street fell into disrepair—whole blocks with their doors and windows bricked up. Then the bulldozers and demolition machines moved in, tearing everything down—with Mr Summers daily to be seen running before the dumper trucks, rescuing chimney pots and fireplaces. Now only the tarmac roads and cobbled alleys remained to show where houses had stood; and the lampposts like black tree stumps after a bush fire.

At the top of the hill, squat and burnt-out like a besieged castle, the old soap factory survived as a ruin. The only other structure was the railway viaduct, which clipped the hillside before striding away into the distance. Every few minutes a train could be counted upon to rattle along it, the windows of the carriages making a neat row of shining squares high up in the sky.

Then Bridie noticed something she'd overlooked before. Dwarfed by the viaduct, its arches soaring over them, she saw people. The type of people Aunt Dolly referred to as *'ne'er-do-wells'*. Tonight the cold drove them to their fires. They reminded Bridie of a lost tribe that had wandered into the city by mistake and, bewildered and knowing no different, had pitched camp here, cooking over their fires as usual.

Soon Bridie noticed more.

What she had accepted as rubbish heaps slowly changed before her eyes, becoming shacks where people lived: each one roughly cobbled together out of planks, crates, plastic, and cardboard—in fact anything that kept out the wet and cold; and dotted around, old wheel-less coaches served as more permanent homes, with their own washing lines and rags at the windows for curtains.

Suddenly Bridie longed for the solid security of a house with all its comforts. It was then she noticed somebody watching her—a woman in a uniform. Thinking her to be a policewoman, Bridie felt a flood of relief and hurried across, only to find the woman's uniform marked out to be a Salvation Army officer.

'You'll have to be quick,' said the woman in a brisk but kindly manner. 'We stop serving in fifteen minutes.'

Gently she ushered Bridie towards a mobile kitchen, lit by a string of naked light bulbs. At one side members of a small brass band were packing away their instruments; and a uniformed man stood holding a banner proclaiming 'Soup, Soap, Salvation'.

The queue before the kitchen waited patiently, even good naturedly. It was made up of all sorts, including families with grubby children and old men shivering in their overcoats. Nobody paid the slightest attention when Bridie joined on at the end.

Food was dispensed through a hatch and from the opening steam billowed. On reaching it, one of the serving ladies said, 'Hello, dear, you're a new face,' before handing Bridie a bowl of soup, a chunk of bread and a tin mug of fiercely hot tea.

'I'm afraid I can't pay right now,' explained Bridie in a small voice. 'I've . . . no money.'

The serving lady laughed, her face shiny from the steam. 'That's all right, dear,' she said. 'Nobody expects you to.'

'But that's *charity*,' said Bridie shocked. 'And Aunt Dolly says never to accept charity. I'll pay what I owe once I get my money back.'

The woman smiled indulgently.

Bridie moved slowly away, balancing her food, and sat on a large lump of concrete. She hadn't been given a spoon, but quite enjoyed drinking her soup straight from the bowl, mopping up afterwards with the bread (she learnt this trick by watching the old men; some even dunked their bread into their teas, although Bridie drew the line at this).

She had nearly finished eating when, from behind, a small black leathery hand shot out, seized her last piece of crust and disappeared with it. The theft was so audacious and took Bridie by such surprise that she didn't have time to see the culprit.

She jumped up in alarm, spilling her tea.

'That's not fair!' she shouted, more angry at being duped than at the loss of the crust.

From the nearest fire she heard a group of men burst out laughing. She could only make out shapes silhouetted against the flames, but knew the men were pointing and laughing at her. Flushed with anger she stormed across as if she were her Aunt Dolly herself wading in with her umbrella. Around the fire she found three men helpless with laughter. On the shoulder of one sat a small monkey happily tearing at the bread and casting it on the ground.

'Your monkey stole my food,' protested Bridie standing before him. 'I think you should teach it to behave or keep it under proper control!' She marvelled at how much she even sounded like Aunt Dolly.

The fellow she had directed her words at, and whom she assumed was the animal's owner, turned and regarded her in the unfriendliest of manners. He was a young man, but looked older because his long fine hair was receding at the front and deep worry lines marked his exposed brow. Like his hair his whiskers were blond but only visible by firelight. He was very fair in all aspects, except his eyes which were exceptionally dark and, at that moment, angry too.

'Spider is not *my* monkey,' he said coldly. 'He is his own person. He does what he wants because *he* chooses to do it. He is as free as any living creature can be, and for you to complain about his behaviour to me is like me complaining about your stupidity to him.'

For a moment Bridie was left speechless. 'Well . . . I think it was a mean thing to do!' she blurted out at last. 'And . . . '

Something came welling up from inside her. It was no longer anger but worry and disappointment and lots of other things all mixed together. She felt sick to the heart. The dry, tearless sobs came before she could prevent them, each one leaving her violently shivering.

'Here, girl, it was only a crust and a bit o' fun,' said one of the other men guiltily. 'We can easily get you another.'

'And don't mind Branwell,' said the third man. 'He was a mite harsh in the way he spoke, but meant no harm by it.'

Branwell scowled and turned away stroking Spider.

'It's n-not th-that.' Bridie's shoulders heaved and her breath broke into short snatches.

'Come and sit down,' invited the third man. 'The fire costs nothing, we can afford to share it. You look half frozen.'

Reluctantly Bridie sat on an old oil drum. 'Th-thank you,' she said, already a little calmer. Reaching into her pocket she pulled out a clean handkerchief carefully wrapped in clingfilm. Seeing the astonishment on the faces of those watching, she shrugged apologetically.

'It's my Aunt Dolly,' she explained. 'She hates dirt and, well, it's just one of her little ways.'

The second man said, 'Sounds the type of woman who

might have strong feelings about you being found in our company.'

'She would!' gasped Bridie. 'She'd probably have all my clothes burned, then scrub me until I was raw . . . Oh, I didn't mean to be rude . . . '

The men laughed (except Branwell who stared into the flames).

'Would I be correct in assuming events have taken a turn for the worse to fetch you up in our midst?' asked the second man, and he tapped the side of his nose. 'Do I smell a story? We likes to hear a good yarn, it helps pass the hours. But first permit me to do the necessaries: Spout Nose is the name—' (He held out his hand very formally and Bridie shook it.) 'Over there is Branwell who isn't saying much for himself at present—nor is Spider the monkey, on account of spider monkeys cannot talk. The other old gentleman is my good friend Selection Box. On the streets nicknames is best stuck to, because when proper names get bandied about they tend to get themselves writ' down on forms and o-fficial documents and other such bits o' paper, then folk can keep their tabs on you.'

'What kind of folk?' asked Bridie.

'Them pen-pushers in their offices,' said Spout Nose darkly. 'That's who.'

Bridie nodded. No further explanations were required to explain how Spout Nose got his nickname, but Selection Box . . . ? He must have guessed her thoughts for, suddenly catching her eye, he gave her such a wide grin that every one of his brown discoloured teeth was revealed like chocolates in a selection box.

Bridie gave a squeal of surprise and burst out laughing; it was some time before she was able to introduce herself back.

'Now, Miss Bridie,' said Spout Nose, 'all pleasantries set aside, I believe you were about to tell us how you happen to be here.'

Bridie looked at him and Selection Box. They were

eagerly leaning towards her. Branwell, pretending no interest, continued to stare deep into the flames.

Turning her back on him, Bridie told her story to Spout Nose and Selection Box. She told them about her Aunt Dolly, who ran a boarding house in Bridlington. She told them about how she had the strictest guest rules in the whole town; and how she once threw out a guest because she found a dirty sock under his bed; and another because he forgot to replace the top on the toothpaste; and yet another because she found biscuit crumbs in his bed.

Selection Box winked at his friend saying, 'Don't think much to our chances if we stayed at that particular establishment.'

Bridie giggled. 'She would chase you away with her broom before you crossed her door step,' she said.

Spout Nose shifted impatiently. 'Carry on,' he urged.

So Bridie told them more about Aunt Dolly's strict ways. About how the carpets and chairs were covered in plastic to protect them against wear; and how the garden had no flowers because flowers attract insects; and how the gas-man had to bring his carpet slippers if he wanted to come in and read the meter.

Spout Nose and Selection Box gasped and tutted where appropriate.

'Oh, Aunt Dolly's not such a bad sort really,' added Bridie. 'She has what she calls *standards*. Then suddenly she became very ill and had to go into hospital. It all happened so quickly. There was hardly any time at all. She wrote to Gramps only a few days ago telling him to expect me.'

'Gramps?' asked Selection Box raising an eyebrow.

'Oh—Mr Summers—he owns the place next to the scrapyard. Or at least I thought he did.'

'What, old Sammy Summers!' cried Selection Box. 'You his grandlittle'un? Well, there's something—eh, Spout Nose? Never knew Sammy Summers had family.'

Spout Nose nodded and even Branwell raised his head.

'Well, we don't visit him very often,' admitted Bridie. 'Aunt Dolly doesn't like coming to the city so usually Gramps comes to our house in Bridlington.'

'But because of your aunt's bad turn you're going to stay with him now?' asked Spout Nose.

Bridie nodded. 'Except when I arrived at the bus station, Gramps wasn't there to meet me as Aunt Dolly had asked in her letter. I thought he must have forgotten and went to his yard. But everything had changed. Gramps was gone—and living in his house are two strange creatures called Amos and Deakin Crickbone. They say they're the caretakers, but I don't believe a word of it.'

Spout Nose and Selection Box blew out their breath and tutted.

Selection Box said, 'Only thing them Crickbones ever taken care of is themselves. You best stay well clear of that pair.'

'But they kept my suitcase!' cried Bridie. 'And all my money. And even if I had them, where could I go?' Timidly she said, 'Do you think I should tell the police?'

An ominous silence met her question. Then Spout Nose said darkly, 'Them's the biggest pen-pushers of the lot.'

'Best think your way through before bringing in the po-lice,' advised Selection Box.

Bridie looked at him. 'If I go to the police they will find Gramps,' she said simply and certainly.

'Ho, will they?' sniffed Spout Nose. 'And what if he doesn't want to be found by no *h*officer of the law, prying into all his comings and goings, writing down his date of birth, and shoe size, and number of time he blinks and coughs and changes his socks in a year?'

'And what about you, miss?' added Selection Box. 'The po-lice will be all kind and concerned, bringing you cups of sweet tea as if you had just had a shock, but soon they'll ask you where *you* live—and what will you say then? "Nowhere at the moment, officer"? Ha, before you knows it you'll be whisked away in a patrol car with its blue lights flashing, to some establishment where young 'uns without mothers and fathers or anyone to take care of 'em have to go.'

'Orphanages,' volunteered Spout Nose. 'That's where they'll put you, an orphanage—prisons for kiddies, more like.'

Bridie's face dropped. 'I hadn't thought of that.'

Spout Nose and Selection Box looked smugly at her. 'Like we say,' said Selection Box, 'best you think your actions through before involving the po-lice.'

'But I have to find Gramps,' cried Bridie. 'He'd never leave his yard. Not without a word. He must be in some kind of trouble—and if he is it's up to me to find him, even if it means living on the streets until I do.'

Spout Nose nodded sympathetically. 'Well, Miss Bridie, it's not such a bad life on the streets if you can take to it.'

'Apart from the wet,' said Selection Box. 'The damp can get in your bones chronic some days.'

'Ah—I grant you that,' agreed Spout Nose.

'And winter can be murderously harsh too.'

'Yes—yes, *some* winters can be quite harsh.'

'Not to mention the dogs,' added Selection Box with a shudder. 'Nasty vicious brutes some of 'em, that would bite you as soon as look at you. Why, some people consider street folk fair game for their dogs. I've lost count the number o' times and places I've been bitten. None of them near my hat wearing end, if you get my meaning.'

Bridie bowed her head. From behind her hair came a soft sniff.

'Selection Box,' sighed Spout Nose. 'Be a good chap and put a sock in it.'

He was madly gesturing at Bridie and Selection Box, realizing he had been tactless, said, 'Oh . . . sock in—put—right away.'

They sat quietly. The fire crackled. Spider picked at his

fur. Then Bridie said, 'I suppose you can't tell me anything about Gramps?'

Spout Nose and Selection Box gravely shook their heads.

'Talk was,' began Selection Box, 'that Sammy Summers had fallen on hard times. Then somehow he got himself mixed up with the Crickbones. Not a wise thing t'do—eh, Spout Nose? Any deal with them is bound to be more crooked than their shadows. Nobody has seen him in a while.'

'What about all Gramps's animals?' asked Bridie.

'Old Mr Summers's cats would have left the moment the Crickbones arrived,' answered Spout Nose. 'On account of neither side can abide the other. The Crickbones would skin a cat as soon as look at it. The brothers claim they're . . . now, what's the word, Selection Box?'

'Algebraic,' replied Selection Box knowledgeably.

Branwell smiled to himself.

'That's it,' said Spout Nose. 'They're algebraic to cats— like some folk are algebraic to spiders or heights.'

'Or soap,' cackled Selection Box.

Spout Nose threw him a disdainful look and went on, 'As for your grandad's chickens, you can rest assured the Crickbones wrung their necks for the pot a long time ago.'

'And what about Trotter, Gramps's old donkey?'

She was surprised when Branwell suddenly turned saying, 'Trotter is safe. *I* can vouch for that. If you come with me I'll even show you and probably find you somewhere safe to sleep for the night too—that is, if you want it.'

Without further explanation or waiting for Bridie's reply, he got up and walked away, Spider riding his back like a jockey.

Bridie shrugged and gazed helplessly at Spout Nose and Selection Box.

'Go with him,' urged Spout Nose, 'Branwell may be

book-learned and moody, but his heart's in the right place. You'll come to no harm with him, I promise.'

Bridie clambered to her feet. 'Thank you and goodbye, Mr Spout Nose and to you Mr Selection Box,' she called running after him.

Chapter Four

In the dark back streets, Bridie felt glad for having Branwell so near. Not that he was good company. At first Bridie felt obliged to keep up beside him and attempt conversation. But, if a nod or shrug didn't suit Branwell, a curt 'Yes' or 'No' did just as well. He strode along, shoulders moodily hunched and hands thrust deep into his pockets.

He thinks I talk too much, Bridie told herself, falling a few paces behind and settling for silence.

Presently they reached a bright main thoroughfare. Without a second glance Branwell waded out into the slow-moving traffic, leaving Bridie fretting on the kerb, going through all the proper motions of crossing the road—instilled into her by Aunt Dolly.

'Well, come on!' called Branwell impatiently.

Cars tooted furiously as Bridie dashed pell-mell to the other side.

Then they plunged into another warren of alleyways, where newspapers blew and steam billowed from the kitchens of Chinese restaurants (along with unbelievably delicious smells). Branwell went striding on ahead and Bridie, growing ever more tired, lagged further and further behind. Suddenly her foot struck a bottle sending it clanking across the cobbles. She knew it was only a bottle, so why did it panic her so?

Like a startled rabbit she began to run. The bitter wind stung her face and ears. She had lost sight of Branwell and Spider. She turned a corner and—

'Ouf!'

She bounced off Branwell's back as he stood waiting for her. He frowned. Spider grinned.

Feeling hopelessly idiotic, Bridie tried to stammer an apology.

'Look,' said Branwell speaking over her. 'I've stopped here because I want to tell you something. I'm not one for prying into other people's business, and certainly don't expect them to pry into mine—but, so you don't think it curious and plague me with endless questions, I've decided to tell you all you need to know about the place where I live.'

He nodded across the derelict wasteland that lay before them to the only building left standing, a once-elegant department store rising in tiled pillars, scrolls, and ornate mouldings above the weeds and rubbish. It stood dark and mysterious—like some shabby grey liner floating helplessly adrift. Its name, visible by the curly golden letters still remaining, or the unweathered stone where they had been, was the Byzantium Bazaar.

'You live there?' gasped Bridie.

Branwell pulled a pained expression. Too late she realized she was not expected to ask questions. *He* would tell her everything she needed to know.

'The Byzantium Bazaar is owned by Miss Firbanks, my mother,' he continued. 'She insists on everyone calling her Miss Firbanks, including me. But *you* won't be calling her anything since *you* shan't meet her.'

'And does she live there with you?' asked Bridie, forgetting herself.

Branwell frowned then nodded. Bridie was intrigued. She couldn't imagine anything living at the Byzantium Bazaar except spiders and mice. Most of its windows were boarded and even from a casual glance it appeared half dilapidated.

'My family were once very well-to-do,' explained Branwell awkwardly. 'Miss Firbanks inherited the business when her father died, not that she ever much cared for it.

Like me her first concern is the welfare of animals.'

Bridie's mouth opened to ask a question. Just in time she remembered and closed it again.

'At first Miss Firbanks tried to run the Bazaar as well as her father had done, despite not having the slightest interest in it. All went well until one day, a customer demanded to see her. He complained that a pen he'd bought didn't work properly. He accused her of cheating him . . . and I think something must have snapped inside Miss Firbanks.'

'Why, what happened?' asked Bridie.

For the first time she saw Branwell smile.

'She tipped a whole bottle of ink over the man's head and had him frog-marched from the store.'

'Serves him right,' said Bridie uncharitably.

'Oh, but that was only the beginning,' said Branwell. 'Next she ordered every other customer out too, threatening them with the fire hose if they didn't get a move on. And when they were gone, she called all the staff together, stuffed everyone's arms with banknotes, wished them goodbye and good-luck, and locked the Bazaar's doors on the public forever. Now she was free to do what she really longed to—'

Bridie's mouth opened.

'That is,' added Branwell quickly, 'turn the Byzantium Bazaar into a refuge for injured, abandoned, and unwanted animals.'

By the time he had finished speaking they were practically there. He took a large key from his pocket and unlocked the bronze outer doors, which were defaced with posters and graffiti.

In her mind Bridie had a clear picture of the formidable Miss Firbanks, and was already a little in awe of her. The shadow of the Bazaar made her whisper. 'When did this happen?'

Branwell pocketed the key. 'Years ago,' he replied. 'That's why I've told you, so you'll understand when we go inside. The store is exactly the same as the day it closed. Everything is still in place and the prices are in pounds, shillings, and pence; and there are sixpences and ten shilling notes in the tills, that look as strange and unfamiliar as foreign money. Come on, I suppose you won't be satisfied until you see for yourself.'

Behind the stout bronze doors lay a set of cobwebby revolving doors. They turned with a dreamlike motion, sweeping Bridie and Branwell through into the darkened ground floor hall.

Bridie shivered. The velvety darkness was a creeping thing, brushing past her like a cat.

Branwell turned on his torch. A beam of weak light appeared which, for Bridie's benefit, he slowly trawled before him. Bridie stood and watched, hardly daring to breathe as ghostly objects slowly paraded themselves before her.

Dust-furred counters and rusting tills.

Ragged mannequins and flaking mirrors.

Cobwebby shelves and stilled clocks.

And the musty air was so thick it might have been water, flooding the vast, silent shopping hall like a gloomy ballroom on a sunken ship. Bridie imagined large hostile fish glowering at her from crevasses in the walls, and shoals of little fish swirling about the ceiling—darting into the great hanging lights as though they were coral draped in weed, not filthy glass smothered in cobwebs.

The darkness rippled as Bridie, led by Branwell, began creeping down an empty aisle, pushing aside the stagnant air as they went. Overhead, cobwebs thickened to resemble garlands of wool slowly rose and fell with the motions of a wave. And everywhere lay signs of hasty abandonment. Like the *Mary Celeste*.

'This way,' beckoned Branwell.

A door led to an outside courtyard and fresh, breathable air. Facing them were loading bays, and on either side the courtyard was divided into pens, each containing a kennel.

The dogs appeared at once. Big dogs, small dogs, old dogs that could barely walk, and excited puppies that scrambled over each other in their haste. And because they recognized Branwell and didn't recognize Bridie, they leapt up either welcoming or threatening, yet all in full voice.

'Hush now!' said Branwell, nervously glancing back at the main block of the store. 'You'll wake Miss Firbanks.'

But the dogs refused to be quiet and Bridie found herself chivvied past them and up some steps, into one of the loading bays. The torchlight fell upon straw. Something stirred.

'Trotter!' exclaimed Bridie, rushing forwards to embrace the bemused donkey's neck. 'Oh, Trotter, how good to see an old friend at last.' She buried her face into his mane, her hand restlessly stroking.

Branwell, leaning against the door, watched her, his eyes dark and thoughtful; and Spider quizzically tilted his head mimicking him.

Soon Trotter grew tired. Unable to hold the weight of his head any longer, Bridie stood aside and the donkey lay down, gave a soft sigh, and went back to sleep.

'He's much greyer than before,' said Bridie as if this was a matter of concern. She picked the straw from her sleeve. 'If only he could talk, perhaps he'd be able to tell us where Gramps has gone . . . ' She stopped as a thought crossed her mind. 'Why is Trotter here with you when he belongs at Gramps's yard?' she asked suspiciously.

'Miss Firbanks bought him off the Crickbones,' replied Branwell. 'She saw them ill treating him in the street and made them sell him to her right there and then. You can be sure they bargained a good price.'

'Poor Trotter,' said Bridie. She bit her bottom lip and gazed back at him.

'Listen,' said Branwell, his tone unexpectedly brisk. 'There's an empty stall next door with enough blankets to keep you warm. It's not ideal, but better than the streets.'

'What about Miss Firbanks?' asked Bridie.

Branwell frowned. 'I don't think it would be a wise thing for you to meet her. She doesn't take well to people—especially strangers. I'll have to think about tomorrow—but you better not get used to the idea of staying here.'

Outside they heard the dogs suddenly renew their clamour. A moment later a tough, rasping voice rang out.

'Branwell! Branwell! Is that you, Branwell?'

'Damn!' muttered Branwell. He held Bridie with his eyes. 'Yes,' he called wearily. 'It's me, Miss Firbanks.'

'Where are you?' demanded the voice bad-temperedly. 'And what on earth are you doing out here at this time of the night?'

Bridie heard feet on the steps and winced. She had not the slightest wish to meet the redoubtable Miss Firbanks.

CHAPTER FIVE

MISS FIRBANKS CAME in holding a hurricane lamp high above her head. She was exactly how Bridie imagined. Tall, unbending, severe. Her silvering hair tightly plaited.

She wore a shapeless pleated skirt (covered in cat hairs), an old cashmere cardigan (wrongly buttoned); and her feet slopped loosely in tennis shoes at least three sizes too large and managing to trail most of their laces behind.

She must have noticed Bridie as soon as she came in, but displayed neither surprise nor the slightest curiosity.

'Is something wrong, Branwell?' she asked in a loud, rasping voice. 'You know I don't like the dogs disturbed once they are down for the night.'

'No, Miss Firbanks,' replied Branwell awkwardly. 'Nothing is wrong.'

'And Trotter? Is he ill? He looks sound enough to me.'

'No, Trotter's fine, Miss Firbanks.'

'Branwell,' said Miss Firbanks stiffening ever so slightly. 'You know my views on *strangers* at the Bazaar.'

Branwell glanced across at Bridie. 'The girl is the granddaughter of Mr Summers,' he said diffidently. 'She didn't know about the Crickbones taking over his yard. I brought her to see Trotter. I . . . I saw no harm in it. I also said she could stay for the night as she has nowhere else to go.'

'Did you indeed?' Miss Firbanks looked stonily unmoved. 'Quite—quite impossible!' She spoke with vehemence. 'Branwell—you know my feelings on the matter. I am deeply displeased by what you have done.'

Then Bridie spoke up saying, 'Please, Miss Firbanks,

29

don't be so angry—not with Branwell, I mean. He thought he was doing his best to help.'

'You were presuming too much, Branwell,' said Miss Firbanks as though Bridie were invisible. She moved to the door saying, 'I expect the situation to be put right immediately.'

'Please, Miss Firbanks—wait!' cried Bridie.

Slowly Miss Firbanks turned and for the first time faced Bridie directly. 'I am waiting,' she said crisply.

'I only want to ask . . . I only want to say . . . ' faltered Bridie. Miss Firbanks started turning away again. 'Please let me stay at the Bazaar, Miss Firbanks. I need to find out what happened to my grandfather. I can only do this if I am here. I know I ask a lot, but if you let me stay I'll work so hard for you in return. I won't be the slightest bit of trouble. Just give me the chance to prove myself. *Please*, Miss Firbanks!'

Miss Firbanks peered hard at the girl, an unfavourable expression on her face.

'What sort of child are you?' she demanded suddenly.

'I . . . I don't understand your question,' stammered Bridie.

Miss Firbanks fixed Bridie with her gaze as if the girl were a fish on the end of a hooked line. 'Of course you do,' she insisted. 'Are you one of those clinging red-eyed creatures that dribble and snivel like some tap that won't turn off? Or are you one of those greedy, devouring types, that is unable to set its eyes on something without demanding to have it? The type that can't comprehend the meaning of the word *enough*. Then again, perhaps you are neither of these. Perhaps you belong to the believes-it-knows-best brigade, who is either deaf to whatever is told it, or will listen carefully in order to do exactly the opposite. No? Then certainly you will flourish on noise. The type of child that makes itself known by a slamming door or with feet hammering upon the stairs—who shouts and bellows, in the misguided belief that whispering is a foreign language it has never quite got to grips with. I repeat—what sort of child are you?'

She glared triumphantly at Bridie, who was left feeling bruised, as if run down by Miss Firbanks's words, or else had them dropped on her one by one like stones. Clearly the woman had no high opinion of children in whatever shape or form.

However, Bridie was determined not to be cowed. Angrily tossing her head she said, 'Why must I be any of these types, Miss Firbanks? As I see it, you just want to go on believing the worst in everybody. It's not right and it's not fair! I should never dream of thinking you the same as the Crickbones just because you are all grown up and *old*. It seems to me, Miss Firbanks, that you know and care more about animals than you do people!'

Miss Firbanks looked poised to speak again, instead an alarming gurgle arose from her chest, which surprised Branwell as much as Bridie—and probably Miss Firbanks herself. It appeared to be laughter. The raucous sound echoed from the walls.

'What impudence!' she cried. 'Calling me old . . . comparing me to those wretched Crickbones.' Abruptly her laughter stopped. 'Do you know how to brush?' she asked.

'Brush?'

'Brush, child—brush! Can I make myself any plainer? Can you brush *hair*?'

Bridie swallowed. 'I suppose . . . Yes, of course I can brush hair.'

'Then follow me.'

Hurricane lamp in hand, Miss Firbanks marched from the room. She said, without looking back, 'Do take that ridiculous smirk off your face, Branwell, it is quite unnecessary.'

Branwell stopped grinning and looked suitably reprimanded.

31

Feeling less brave than a moment before, Bridie followed Miss Firbanks back into the store.

'Pay close attention to the things I tell you as we go along,' instructed Miss Firbanks. 'I do not enjoy repeating myself, and do not suffer fools gladly.'

'Y-yes, Miss Firbanks.'

They climbed the Bazaar's main staircase. It was marble and swept down like a frozen river. Bridie sharply drew back her hand from the touch of the banister. It was cold and clammy, as if a sweat lay upon the stone; and Miss Firbanks's lamp revealed slime glistening upon the walls and places where the plaster had crumbled away to the brickwork.

Miss Firbanks talked incessantly, but Bridie paid little attention. She was too busy gazing around and wondering what lay behind the wide doors, which they came to at each landing, and which led away to a different department. She felt like an archaeologist in a pyramid or some other undisturbed tomb—

'I said are you listening, child?'

'Oh yes . . . yes, Miss Firbanks,' said Bridie coming out of her thoughts.

'Well then, open the door.'

They stood on a landing close to the top of the Bazaar. Bridie had just time to glance up at a little brass plaque, now dull with grime, and read *Bedding Department*, before opening the door and following Miss Firbanks through.

The sight of row upon row of empty beds stretching away into the undisturbed darkness greeted her, giving her a sense of unease. It was as if she was trespassing upon a ghostly dormitory or an abandoned hospital; and Bridie saw that some beds were swathed in cobwebs like mosquito nets, while some mattresses were riddled with holes where mice had built nests. The darkness swirled around Miss Firbanks's lamp as she crossed to the only made-up bed and sat down. She loosened her plait, and ruffled her marvellously long hair until it fell wildly about her.

'Show me what you can do, child,' she ordered motioning at a silver brush by her side.

Bridie clambered on to the bed behind her, picked up the brush and made one or two timorous strokes with it.

'Much harder, child!' cried Miss Firbanks. 'Do you think you can hurt me? Harder! You're doing no good at all.'

Bridie brushed and brushed until her arm ached and the old woman was chuckling to herself. Only it wasn't a proper laugh, but more a sound of contentment—like a cat purring. Gradually her stiffly held head lolled to one side and she breathed out a long sigh.

For a while Bridie continued to brush, the strokes growing less and less severe until she stopped altogether.

'Miss Firbanks?' she whispered.

A snore replied.

Carefully climbing down off the bed, Bridie went and stood in front of the old woman. Her hair curtained her face. Drawing it back, Bridie saw that her eyes were closed and she was sleeping contentedly.

Bridie hesitated, wondering if she should wake her, but as this seemed unnecessary, she carefully arranged a quilt around Miss Firbanks's shoulders, then went and hunted amongst the shelves until she had discovered enough blankets for herself.

The hiss of the hurricane lamp died abruptly the moment Bridie turned it off and, crawling on to one of the vacant beds nearby, she curled up and within a few minutes she too had fallen asleep.

Chapter Six

A GREY, COLD dawn broke over the city. But the boarded windows of the Byzantium Bazaar were tight, leaking no light, and Bridie slept on through the unbroken darkness. Yet, while she lay sleeping, a restless, haunting sound crept into her head. She opened her eyes and the sound hung before her in the air. She lay still wondering what it might mean. Suddenly she realized. It was the sound of cats— many cats—yawping and yowling upon the stairs.

Miss Firbanks finished braiding her hair, held up her lamp and said, 'Look lively, child. Don't you hear us summoned to our first duty?'

Yawning and still half asleep, Bridie stumbled after her, out on to the marble stairway. There she was pulled up sharp, staring in astonishment. Down to the darkness of the next landing the steps were thronged and heaving with cats. Bridie had never seen so many at once before. Perhaps they numbered two hundred. Perhaps more.

Holding Miss Firbanks in their sight the cats now surged forwards, their noise so unbearably harsh and loud that Bridie covered her ears. Miss Firbanks, however, laughed and clapped her hands delightedly.

'Listen . . . my very own dawn chorus,' she declared. 'And see, child, they come bearing gifts.'

At first Bridie didn't understand. Then she noticed certain of the cats pushing ahead of the cluster, each gently gripping a mouse or rat in its mouth. Lowering their heads, the cats softly placed their offerings at Miss Firbanks's feet and respectfully backed away again.

Bridie was horrified—more so with Miss Firbanks who

acted as if she couldn't be better pleased, throwing up her hands in mock surprise and thanking each cat by name. It was not how Aunt Dolly would have reacted!

Soon Miss Firbanks grew impatient. She scanned the cat army, apparently in search of something. Surely it can't be for more dead mice, thought Bridie.

'I don't see him,' Miss Firbanks was fretting. 'Where is he? Where is your lord—that prince of prowlers . . . ? Ah, he approaches.'

As she spoke, Bridie sensed an uneasy stirring amongst the cats and saw them draw aside until a path lay clearly defined through the middle of them. Sauntering up it came, a large white cat with chocolate paws. He stared straight ahead, his eyes green and almond shaped, his regal face expressionless. He was disdainful of the company of his fellow cats, and should any of them so much as brush against him, he spat and hissed and his dense fur rose—and that hiss was as threatening as a rattlesnake's warning.

'Ahh,' cooed Miss Firbanks. 'Good morning, Shah.'

The great cat launched himself into Miss Firbanks's arms, stretching himself to his full length and throbbing with purrs. Miss Firbanks flushed with pleasure.

'Child,' she said, 'step forward and make yourself known to the Shah of Purrshire, first of his kind at the Byzantium Bazaar. He rules my other cats, keeping them in order. I expect you to give him your full respect.'

'Yes, Miss Firbanks,' said Bridie. She remembered what Gramps had once told her. That if there is a king cat, make peace with it and all other cats will fall into line.

Miss Firbanks lifted Shah a little higher. His eyes widened to study Bridie in a lazy, disinterested way. It made Bridie feel uncomfortable and her hand, half risen to stroke the thick creamy fur, wavered uncertainly before going back down to her side.

'Since proving to me you are adequate with a brush,' continued Miss Firbanks, 'your first task each morning is to groom the great Shah. Be warned, I shall be most displeased if ever I find a knot or burr in his coat. And, when that is done, I expect you to help me feed his hungry subjects.'

Bridie suddenly found the cat thrust upon her, and before she could say another word, Miss Firbanks marched away, drawing the multitude of cats after her, their silky movements like liquid—a dam-burst of cats pouring down the steps and washing about Miss Firbanks's feet. In seconds they were gone.

Bridie blinked at Shah; he glowered back at her.

He lay rigid and uncooperative in her arms and through her sleeve she felt the points of his claws reminding her they were there. Staggering beneath his weight, she managed to manoeuvre him into the bedding department and laid him on the nearest bed. She looked around. The only brush was the silver one she had used the previous night.

She shrugged. 'Oh well, as long as Miss Firbanks doesn't mind . . . '

Turning, she was startled to find Shah watching her through slitted eyes. In little flicks his tail beat upon the bed, demonstrating the cat equivalent to human finger-tapping.

When Bridie went to brush him, he slipped on to his back.

'Oh, come on, you stupid thing—Ow!'

The needle sharp teeth sank deep. Bridie leapt back. Shah went streaking through the door.

Bridie discovered Miss Firbanks in the old electrical department. It took no great work of detection, but was simply a matter of following the noise. Branwell was there too. He glanced up from opening a can of cat food and grunted.

Brandishing a wooden spoon, Miss Firbanks cried, 'Come along, child, all hands to the pumps.'

This was easier said than done. Feeding cats covered every inch of the floor, crowding four or five to a dish; and were also upon the bulky television sets and antiquated twin tubs. Those *not* feeding were staging ambushes, jumping down from the radiograms on to the unwary passer-by; or were using the upright vacuum cleaners as scratching posts; or merely patrolled the various shelves of rusting toasters and cobwebby food mixers. Claw and spitting fights were common and cat tempers, already frayed, were further aggravated by Spider, who couldn't resist the temptation of pulling the odd tail or two.

Picking her way through with extreme care, Bridie at last joined Miss Firbanks and Branwell at the counter. Hungry cats nosed in on all sides. Angrily Miss Firbanks swept them away as if they were nothing more than old dusters.

'What sort of impression did you create on Shah?' she called above the wailing and hissing.

'He bit me,' Bridie shouted back.

Miss Firbanks threw up her head to give a brief explosive laugh. 'What did you expect, child? Kindness? Always remember, he is a king and you are nothing more than a lowly servant.'

As with Miss Firbanks's affections, the rest of the animals followed the cats of the Byzantium Bazaar. For Bridie it became one endless whirl of feeding, watering, grooming, exercising, and cleaning. But she began to learn a little more about the Bazaar itself, since different animals were quartered on different levels; while the haberdashery department, half-way up the building, served as a sick bay. Here Miss Firbanks, suitably kitted for the part in a long white apron and wellington boots, had Bridie grinding powders, measuring medicines, fetching bandages, and applying ointments. Everything was done at a rush, with Miss Firbanks barking out orders and sweeping on to the next thing before Bridie realized she had gone.

About mid-day Bridie drew her hand across her brow and said, 'Does she never stop?'

'Never,' replied Branwell.

'But . . . when do we eat?' Bridie remembered she'd had no breakfast and precious little else the day before.

'Miss Firbanks has certain strong notions on food and eating,' explained Branwell. 'Not only is she a strict vegetarian—we both are in fact—but she thinks we eat far too much and can make do on one set meal a day.'

'One!' Bridie's face fell.

'Luckily I don't happen to share that view,' grinned Branwell, and he whispered, 'Try and slip away downstairs in about fifteen minutes.'

If Miss Firbanks considered the bedding department as her own private domain, the same might be said of Branwell and the camping department.

It was easy to understand why he chose to live there. He had a ready-made home in a small tent upon a display stand, complete with plastic grass, a plastic campfire and a plastic palm tree for Spider to climb. Altogether it resembled a little castaway island. Over it, like a cloud, hovered a sign announcing: 'Welcome to the great outdoors—yours for less than twelve guineas'.

Branwell looked up the moment he heard the door open.

'Quickly—come in,' he called. 'Before Miss Firbanks sees you!' He sounded like a guilty schoolboy.

The smell of cooking drew Bridie to his side. Several camping stoves were hissing away with pans bubbling over them. Bridie stretched herself out on the plastic grass with Spider, watching as Branwell carefully adjusted the flames.

'I'm starved,' she said. 'I can't believe that Miss Firbanks eats just once a day. I wouldn't last a week.'

'Oh, it's true all right,' said Branwell. 'But that's not the half of it—each day it's always the same thing. An incredibly disgusting concoction she calls her universal vegetable hash. Ugh! Be warned, never go to dinner if Miss Firbanks invites you.'

They laughed. Branwell seemed much more relaxed today and Bridie thought how pleasant he looked when not scowling.

'Here,' he said thrusting a plate at her. 'Beans, instant mash, tomatoes, and crisps. I didn't promise I was the best of cooks. Try to use the crisps to scoop up the rest, that way it saves on knives and forks.'

Bridie ate hungrily, but she hadn't forgotten there was something serious she needed to discuss too.

'Branwell,' she said slowly. 'How do I find Gramps? Where do I start? Should I try asking the Crickbones again?'

'It's no use trying to squeeze anything out of them,' said Branwell licking his fingers. 'And if it turns out they *are* involved in something unsavoury, you can be sure they've covered up their tracks pretty well.'

'So—?'

Branwell looked at her thoughtfully. 'If anyone knows anything it'll be the street people,' he said. 'They know everything that happens in the city. The only trouble is they're a suspicious lot and they don't speak freely to strangers. They have to get to know you, which can take time.'

Bridie put down her plate, her appetite suddenly gone.

'Tell you what,' said Branwell trying to sound cheerful. 'Each evening I go out on what I call my night patrol, rounding up any strays from the streets. Come with me. That way the street people'll get to know your face and learn to trust you.'

'Thanks, Branwell,' smiled Bridie.

Suddenly Spider started acting strangely, jumping up and down and waving his arms.

'Quickly!' cried Branwell. 'Hide your plate—'

But it was too late.

'Ah, here you are!' hallooed Miss Firbanks bursting through the doors. 'I've been hunting high and low for you both . . . ' She stopped, her mouth twitching with disapproval. 'What is this spectacle I see before me? Branwell, be so good as to explain yourself.'

'Explain, Miss Firbanks . . . ? What?' Branwell tried sounding innocent but failed miserably.

Miss Firbanks held up an empty, crumpled packet between her thumb and first finger. '*Salt and vinegar flavoured crisps*,' she read, pronouncing each word with a terrible clarity.

'Er, they were for me, Miss Firbanks,' said Bridie. 'I was so hungry I had to eat something.'

'Naturally,' conceded Miss Firbanks. 'You are a healthy, growing creature. But that is still no reason for Branwell to poison you.' Disdainfully dropping the packet she said, 'Tonight you may dine with me and understand the true meaning of *nourishment*.'

Remembering Branwell's previous dire warning, Bridie began stammering excuses.

'I eat at seven,' said Miss Firbanks firmly. 'Don't be late. I cannot abide lateness.'

And she promptly turned and left.

CHAPTER SEVEN

AT FIVE TO seven, Bridie started up the stairs to the top of the Byzantium Bazaar. It was a steep climb—or perhaps just felt that way because her heart wasn't in it. She shielded her candle from the fierce draughts, occasionally pausing to sniff the air, hoping to catch some delicious aroma drifting down to meet her and perk up her dragging feet. But all she ever smelt was damp and mould.

At last the staircase reached the topmost landing. Facing her stood a stout mahogany door. She cleared the cobwebs off a small brass plaque and read *Directors' Room*. This was the place. She knocked nervously, waited a moment, then went in.

The panelled room was as dusty as any at the Bazaar, and cobwebs all but hid the portraits of Miss Firbanks's forefathers (and the store's previous owners) in their heavy gilt frames, but dimly discernible were stern men with monocles or mutton chop whiskers and the vague look of Miss Firbanks about them. In the centre of the room a long table was surrounded by many chairs. The table-top dust was thick enough to show the crisscrossing trails of passing cats, also overlapping rings revealing where plates had stood. A candelabra at the centre gave out a thin wavering light, catching silver, crystal, and china—the finest of their kind, and all borrowed from the different departments downstairs.

At the room's furthest end, the wall was entirely of glass. Bridie crept up to it. Beyond the roosting pigeons, the city's lights twinkled distantly, like a port viewed from out at sea.

'I never bothered to have them boarded up,' said a

41

familiar cracked voice. 'We're too high up for the vandals to reach and it would be such a pity to lose the view.'

Miss Firbanks swept past, banging a covered dish on the table. 'Sit yourself down, child. There's no ceremony here.' And when Bridie was perched upon one of the dusty chairs, the old woman leaned across and said, 'I suppose Branwell informed you of my rather limited menu?'

'Er . . . I think he did mention something,' replied the girl tactfully.

'Rubbish! He told you exactly, no doubt finding it highly amusing too.'

As Miss Firbanks spoke the candles swirled in her wake. She slammed down the knives and forks, then crashed down the dish's lid, steam uncoiling into her face like an angry genie.

'My motto,' she declared, clattering a ladle, 'is nutritious before delicious.'

'My Aunt Dolly says we all need three square meals a day.'

Miss Firbanks stopped dead to stare at the girl. 'From what you tell me, your Aunt Dolly sounds an incredibly ill-informed and silly woman. Now pass me your plate.'

Bridie's mouth fell open. She had heard her aunt described as 'worthy', 'respectable', and even 'decent' before now (usually in tones of breathless admiration). But *silly* . . . ! She handed her plate across automatically.

Scooping up some grey coloured stuff, Miss Firbanks gave a fine Wedgwood plate several hefty whacks until the stuff *glopped* on to it. The plate (which was as chipped and cracked as the rest of the china) came skimming over the table-top, spinning to a halt before Bridie. Steam rose—but no real smell accompanied it, beyond something vaguely reminiscent of . . . well . . . washing powder.

'This recipe is of my own devising,' said Miss Firbanks brandishing a knife. 'The result of proper scientific enquiry. It is based upon the haricot bean which, to my mind, is a seriously underestimated source of nourishment. Do you know, child, I haven't suffered a single cold since I first started eating my universal vegetable hash nearly thirty years ago? Begin—begin, it requires some chewing.'

Some of the grey *stuff* stuck to the prongs of Bridie's fork and she raised it to her lips. Reluctantly she took the smallest of nibbles. The *stuff* seemed instantly to swell in her mouth, sticking to her teeth, refusing to be swallowed. She gulped down some water.

'That's right,' said Miss Firbanks approvingly. 'Drink plenty of water. People don't, you know—but they should. It flushes out the blood. Now eat up and you shall have some more.'

Just then Bridie was relieved to hear a knock at the door.

'What is it, Branwell?' called out Miss Firbanks. 'You know I hate being disturbed when I'm chewing my food.'

Branwell's grinning face showed itself around the door, with Spider's a little higher up.

'Sorry, Miss Firbanks,' he said. 'I've come for Bridie. She offered to come with me on the night patrol.'

'This is too bad, Branwell. Can't you see the poor child is eating? I'm educating her stomach.'

'I've heard there's a couple of stray dogs loose in Union Street,' said Branwell. 'It sounds pretty urgent.'

'We'd better go right away,' said Bridie leaping up.

'Yes—yes,' agreed Miss Firbanks suddenly concerned. 'The traffic in Union Street can be particularly bad—poor things'll be witless with fear.'

At the door Bridie hesitated. 'Thank you for inviting me to dinner, Miss Firbanks,' she said. 'I wonder . . . could I ask one more favour?'

'What child?'

'All my things—they were stolen by the Crickbones and I haven't any other clothes. Please, if you don't think it wrong of me to ask, could I borrow some new ones from the store?'

'Yes—yes. What do I want with old clothes? Just get yourself along to Union Street as quickly as possible.'

On the stairs Branwell and Bridie burst out laughing.

'Thanks for rescuing me,' said Bridie.

'Here,' said Branwell thrusting a large fruit and nut chocolate bar at her. 'So you don't starve.'

They shared it, feeding titbits to Spider.

Reaching the landing outside the women's and girls' department Branwell stopped, but Bridie continued down the stairs.

'Hey! Where are you going?' he called after her. 'I thought you wanted some clothes?'

'Have you seen how horrible the fashions were when Miss Firbanks closed the store?' Bridie's reproachful voice came floating back. And ten minutes later she reappeared dressed entirely in plain boys' clothes. Jeans, shirt, jumper, and duffle coat. Smelling musty but still quite serviceable.

'You look like a boy now,' said Branwell. 'Although I'm not sure if Spider knows what to make of you.'

Bridie ran her hand down the monkey's back. 'It's all for a good cause, Spider,' she said softly. 'Now, let's go and see if we can find any news about Gramps.'

CHAPTER EIGHT

DEAR AUNT DOLLY

I hope you are well and getting much better all the time. We are all fine here. I am sending you a postcard of a statue of the famous Queen Victoria in the municipal gardens. It is just like the one in the picture at home, the one you like to dust. Will write again soon.

Love Bridie xx

p.s. When I grow up I want to work with animals.

Bridie wrote the postcard care of the hospital, to keep Aunt Dolly from worrying. Bridie wouldn't—couldn't—lie, not to Aunt Dolly. Yet if her aunt presumed the *we* in the postcard to mean Gramps and Bridie herself, well, so much the better.

Bridie wondered what would happen if she wrote the truth. *Dear Aunt Dolly . . . Gramps disappeared into thin air . . . am living with complete strangers in a condemned building . . . spend most evenings with tramps* (that's what Aunt Dolly called them). It would probably set the monitors by her bedside beeping and flashing and bring the nurses rushing in with tablets to calm her down.

Two weeks had now passed since Bridie first arrived in the city. Fourteen nights. And although on every single one of those nights she had been to Soap Hill asking after Gramps, she was still no nearer to finding out what had happened to him, not by a single clue.

Some street people she asked shook their heads and were done with the matter.

Some, like Spout Nose and Selection Box, airily

promised to 'ask around' on her behalf. Some were blunt, almost to the point of hostile, coming back with variations of Snail's, 'Ain't seen nuffin'. Don't know nuffin'. Don't bovver no one.'

'It's useless,' complained Bridie bitterly. 'They'll never tell me anything.'

Branwell smiled sympathetically. 'Secrecy is just their way of protecting themselves,' he said. 'Like nicknames. Strangers are always viewed with suspicion. Don't forget some take to the streets in order to escape their troubles. There is a kind of honour in keeping silent.'

'But he's my grandfather!'

'They don't know that. They think it is rather strange that a girl dressed as a boy should be asking so many questions.'

Now Bridie was furious with him because he was so calm and reasonable. He put his arm around her.

'All I'm trying to tell you, Bridie, is it will take a little time. That's all.'

Meanwhile Bridie's life grew more settled, falling in with the routine of the Bazaar. It started early each morning with the grooming of Shah and ended each evening on the streets, rounding up strays, Bridie ever hopeful of catching some loose titbit of gossip concerning her grandfather. In between hours, Miss Firbanks worked her like she worked herself.

Often Bridie thought of the Bazaar, with its animals on every floor, as a great stone Ark. Not that Miss Firbanks was a benign Mrs Noah figure at its helm. No, rather Miss Firbanks was a female Blackbeard, bellowing out orders and terrifying local tradesmen with her raids on their shops, demanding bones and scraps for the animals.

Apart from her beloved cats, the dogs in the kennels outside and dear old Trotter, Miss Firbanks's waifs and strays came in all shapes and sizes. There were rabbits, goats, chinchillas, foxes, ducks, guinea pigs, assorted reptiles, and Samson the blind owl. And if these weren't enough, there was also a host of stowaways. The rats and mice were a destructive nuisance, but Miss Firbanks showed a touching fondness for the bats in the carpet department.

And most nights some new creature would be borne home to join the crew. A cast-out dog. A bag of kittens thrown into the canal to drown. A bad-tempered crow, its wing peppered with gun shot. No animal was ever turned away. There was room enough for them all on the S.S. Byzantium Bazaar.

One cold, frosty night, with the mist rising at the foot of Soap Hill, Bridie and Branwell were making their way back home. It had been an unsuccessful patrol in all respects, with neither strays nor word from the street people about Mr Summers.

Bridie was quiet. Branwell glanced at her. He knew she was close to despair. He lifted Spider from his shoulder and placed him on to Bridie's. Spider was a great comforter—he always sensed what to do. He clung tightly to Bridie's neck and she stroked him, whispering in his ear all the things she was unable to tell anyone else.

The wind blew raw and they hurried on, cutting down the alleyway that ran between the railway and the old nail factory. Suddenly Branwell stopped. 'Listen,' he said.

They stood together listening.

'It's a cat,' said Bridie.

'In some sort of trouble,' said Branwell. 'Sounds as if it's on the railway line.'

They rushed further down the alley until they found a hole in the fence.

'I'll go,' said Bridie. 'It's too small for you.'

'Be careful,' warned Branwell, but Bridie had already squeezed through the hole, taking Spider with her.

Behind the fence, Bridie discovered that the railway embankment sloped steeply away in a litter-strewn tangle of briars and elders, that was all but impenetrable. Thorns tore at her clothes and snagged her hair. She stumbled, muttering the curses Branwell used when Miss Firbanks wasn't in earshot.

She was about to turn back and find some easier route when, with a sickening jolt, her feet skidded from under her and she struck the ground hard.

Winded and unable to cry out, she went ploughing through the undergrowth at a gathering speed, until, somewhere near the bottom, she came to a halt. Before her the railway lines glowed palest silver on a bed of stones.

Her hand touched fur. 'Spider,' she gasped. 'Are you all right?'

Judging by the way Spider was running his paws over her face, it seemed, in his own way, he was asking the same question of her.

Close by, the cat put up its cry once more. Before Bridie could move, she heard gruff voices and lay still, listening.

'Get a stone.'

'A big stone?'

'A big stone.'

'Knock it from the tree!'

'I have a stick.'

'Use it! Use it!'

Had Bridie known no better, she would have sworn it was one person talking to and answering himself. Now her eyes were fully used to the darkness, she saw the crooked, dried-out figures of Amos and Deakin Crickbone. Like each other's shadow, they stood beneath a tree, in whose branches lodged a soft white shape.

'Shah!' mouthed Bridie in horror.

'Let's get it! Let's get it!' Deakin was shrieking. 'Let's kill the devil cat. I can hardly breathe with it so near to me!' He sneezed violently.

'I told you, get a stone.'

'*You* get a stone—I have my stick.'

'A stone is better than a stick.'

'But you don't have a stone!'

The brothers appeared on the point of coming to blows, but then, with perfect timing, turned and directed their loathing back at Shah.

Bridie watched feeling utterly powerless, wondering what she could do against two men. She didn't notice Spider grow tense in her arms. It startled her when he fought free and bounded away.

'Spider, come back!' she hissed. But already he had leapt across the railway lines.

In the shadow of the far-side embankment, Bridie lost sight of him altogether. Only when Deakin screamed at the top of his voice did she again see Spider, running up Deakin's back to pull his bowler hat down hard over his eyes, sending him blundering into Amos, who screamed at precisely the same moment as his brother, even though he had no cause to.

Inspired by Spider's example, Bridie gave a shout, broke cover and charged down the tracks, bounding from sleeper to sleeper.

What a sight she must have looked, with her clothes torn ragged and her hair a tangle of twigs and leaves. Her sudden appearance certainly had a dramatic effect on the Crickbones. They clung to each other, their mouths slavering and eyes bulging.

They looked so comical that Bridie wanted to laugh, but swallowing it back let out a long moan instead, confirming the Crickbones' worst fears about this unearthly creature that had risen from the ground, and was fast bearing down on them. They turned and fled, falling over each other in their panic.

Feeling something spring nimbly upon her back, Bridie whispered, 'Well done, Spider.' She held out her arms to catch Shah as he unhurriedly dropped from the branches above, her legs almost buckling beneath his weight. Shah pushed his head under her chin, purring madly.

But it was not yet time for congratulations. A little further off, the Crickbones had regained their composure and their glares at Bridie were like poisoned beams.

'It's that girl!'

'What girl?'

'The one who came snooping.'

'The one with the cock-and-bull story?'

'Yes—yes—that girl.'

'What is she doing here?'

'Spying on us.'

'Spying?'

'Watching everything we does.'

'Perhaps . . . perhaps she knows.'

'No—no. How could she?'

'Easy if she's a spy.'

'Which she is.'

'We ought to find out.'

'Yes.'

'We ought to stop her meddling.'

'Yes—yes.'

'We ought to teach her never to spy no more.'

Bridie didn't like the way the brothers came edging forwards as they spoke. Desperately she searched around for a means of escape. The embankment? No, she'd never beat her way back to the top. Down the line then? Impossible. How could she hope to side step both Amos *and* Deakin? She glanced behind at the only way left and saw the tunnel.

Without a second thought, she turned and ran straight towards it. The Crickbones pursued her, snarling like dogs.

Under the tunnel's arch the air was suddenly damp, the darkness complete. No longer able to see to run, Bridie felt her way with her toes. Sleeper . . . Stones . . . Sleeper. The

Crickbones' abuse echoed in her ears—but at least they hadn't followed. They were too afraid. Soon even their voices fell silent. Distantly, Bridie made out a patch of grey light, marking the tunnel's furthest end. It seemed so far away and she knew she must keep her nerve.

Sleeper . . . Stones . . . Sleeper.

As she went she remembered her voice.

'We can reach it,' she told Shah and Spider in an unconvincingly cheerful tone. 'I only have to walk and I'm there—and anybody can walk. It's simply a matter of putting one foot after the other. Easy. Sleeper . . . Stones . . . Sleeper.'

Then she heard a sound.

The animals also heard it. Spider's grip tightened. Shah lay tense like a coiled spring.

The sound grew steadily louder, making a kind of eerie metallic music. It came from the railway tracks.

They were singing!

Bridie knew what it meant and what danger she was in. But she couldn't go back, even if there was time. Her legs had turned rigid with fear.

Bright headlights now swung into view at the tunnel's opposite end. Two powerful beams lighting up every brick and stone and the brown stalactites secretly growing from the roof.

'Branwell!' she screamed—her shrill voice distorted by echoes.

Frantically she pushed against the curving brickwork. Moulding her body to the shape of the arch. Squeezing herself back as if hoping an invisible door would swing open and let her fall safely through.

The train's headlights dazzled. She was as blind as when the tunnel had lain in darkness. Noise filled her ears. Once more she opened her mouth to scream. But the train was there: a monster sucking the air from her.

A terrifying clatter.

A gash of light.

A roaring wind.

Darkness.

The metallic song dying on the tracks and a red light fading into the distance.

Bridie's body unclenched itself and sagged with relief. She thought she was trembling with shock. It took a moment to realize that it was Shah. He was purring.

'Bridie! Bridie! Are you there? Are you hurt?'

Never was Bridie so glad to hear another's voice.

'Here, Branwell . . . ! I'm all right—we all are!'

CHAPTER NINE

BACK AT THE Bazaar, they met Miss Firbanks on the stairs. Bridie told her at once what had happened and was gratified to see the growing look of horror on the old woman's face. Her mouth hung open and she pressed her finger-tips so hard against her cheeks that little white spots remained when she took her hands away.

'Those awful Crickbones! Terrible Crickbones! Evil Crickbones!' she cried with distress and passion, her hands clenching into fists. 'And you, dear child . . . How brave you were . . . How very brave and daring . . . '

Bridie gasped with surprise as Miss Firbanks's lips swooped down, touching both her cheeks with a brief kiss as dry as paper.

She felt Shah lifted from her at the same time, then Miss Firbanks swept off, white fur overflowing her arms. 'I will not forget this, child,' she called back. 'You shall know my gratitude.'

When she was gone Branwell turned to Bridie and shrugged. 'Cocoa and biscuits?' he suggested hopefully.

'No thanks, Branwell,' smiled Bridie. 'I feel too whacked all of a sudden. I think I'll turn in now if you don't mind. Goodnight.'

'Goodnight.'

She listened to Branwell's feet tip-tapping down the stairway to his tent, before slowly climbing in the opposite direction, to the toy department where her own camp bed was set up.

The grey unsold toys were waiting for her when she entered, and along the shelves glass eyes suddenly gleamed in the candlelight, seeming to make the dusty dolls and teddy bears spring watchfully alive. Sometimes Bridie thought the presence of the old toys quite sinister, other times she found it comforting. Tonight, however, she did not bother considering the matter at all. Kicking off her boots, she climbed into bed fully dressed against the cold. She lay listening to the mice scurrying underneath the floorboards, and, no longer troubled by it, fell asleep.

'Do you hear me, child?'

Bridie awoke, shielding her eyes from a glaring light at the foot of her bed.

She raised herself upon an elbow, squinting up her eyes until it made her look angry.

'Miss . . . Miss Firbanks?'

'Rise up, child.'

'Is something wrong?'

Miss Firbanks, Bridie now saw, stood dressed in a long nightgown, wellington boots, and an army greatcoat. Her face was flushed with excitement.

'It is my wish to show you something, child,' she whispered. 'Something no one else has ever seen before. Not even Branwell.' She gave a nervous giggle. 'I call it my Chamber of Horrors.'

She held up the hissing hurricane lamp and beckoned.

Mystified, and with feelings of apprehension, Bridie slid out of bed and tugged on her boots. When she stood up, Miss Firbanks had gone. She ran out on to the landing. Miss Firbanks stood there waiting for her. Slowly she turned, raising a finger to her lips.

Then, step by step, she led the way down, not a word passing between them, until it was too late for Bridie to ask the questions she most wanted to know—the silence had lasted too long. Like a child, Miss Firbanks savoured her control of the moment, walking with an uncharacteristic lack of haste. She paused to gaze back at the girl, the bright yellow light illuminating her exhilarated expression, her frizzled hair as incandescent as a halo. In that one brief moment, Bridie sensed the mystery's fullness and shuddered.

She heard the old woman laugh softly and go on again in silence.

Presently they reached the broad sweeping foot of the stairs. Miss Firbanks lowered her head, leading Bridie to a small door concealed beneath them, tucked away from public view.

Abruptly the old woman seized Bridie's wrist. 'Child,' she whispered fiercely, 'this is *our* little secret. Nobody else must know. Promise me you'll not breathe a word of what lies behind this door to another living soul.'

Bridie's voice caught in her throat. Her words came thickly. 'I promise,' she said.

Reassured, Miss Firbanks touched Bridie's cheek and, pulling a key from her pocket, unlocked the door. Plain brick steps and an iron banister descended into absolute darkness. Bridie shivered.

'Cold?' asked Miss Firbanks.

Bridie stroked her arms and nodded.

'That is because we are going deep into the earth, child, where it is always cold—even in summer—and requires to be so, for what I choose to keep down here.'

At the bottom of the stairs a room slowly opened out, its walls limed and flaking and carrying service pipes, with here and there a wheeled valve. The centre space was dominated by an enormous boiler, the coal brought in to feed it sloping away, no longer black, but white with dust. Behind the boiler, a caged corner marked the bottom of the old lift shaft and was half filled with rubbish.

These things Bridie took in at a glance. Then smaller details caught her eye: playing cards mouldering on a box for a table, a shovel growing rusty in the coal and, on a nail, the braided uniform of a doorman left to rot until its epaulettes were unravelling like coarse, brown string. Bridie saw all these things and more, but nothing that fitted Miss Firbanks's previous description, *Chamber of Horrors*.

The old woman thrust the hurricane lamp at her, urging, 'Go see—see for yourself, child.'

Not a little puzzled, Bridie accepted the lamp and stepped out into the room.

'I don't know what you want me to see,' she called a moment later.

'*Look*, child!' snapped Miss Firbanks impatiently, watching from the darkness of the stairs. 'Use your eyes.'

Suddenly Bridie noticed three clothes rails pushed back into an alcove. Hanging on the rails were a great number of zippered bags.

'That's it, child,' called Miss Firbanks encouragingly, as she crossed towards them.

Putting down the lamp, Bridie unzipped the nearest bag and slid her hand inside. The deep, cool, velvety touch of fur made her shiver in delight.

'Why, Miss Firbanks,' she cried out without thinking. 'It's beautiful!'

'*Beautiful!*' repeated the old woman bitterly. 'Living creatures cruelly trapped and barbarically slaughtered so a giddy girl like you can burble such nonsense. I brought you here so that—'

'I'm sorry,' cried Bridie. 'I didn't mean any harm. I just couldn't help myself . . . '

'Hmm.' Miss Firbanks reined back her anger. 'In my father's day,' she said, 'the Byzantium Bazaar was renowned for the quality and rareness of its furs. Mink, ermine, lynx, leopard, beaver, sable, ocelot. You required a special appointment simply to view them. They were not meant for the hoi polloi.'

Bridie unzipped another bag and stroked the soft grey chinchilla fur inside. 'They must have cost a lot of money,' she observed.

Miss Firbanks laughed hollowly. 'They did, child, they did—an honest man's wages for a year, perhaps longer. But that is as nothing compared to their worth today. Some of the animals, whose skins hang before you, have been practically hunted from the wild. Some verge on the brink of extinction. Rarity is an expensive and desirable thing, child. Any one coat might command thousands of pounds. Yet I would rather take a knife and slash every last coat to ribbons before I would consider selling any.'

'Why don't you,' asked Bridie, 'if you hate them so much? After all they do belong to you.'

The old woman considered this, then replied, 'I find it good for the soul to come down and gaze on them from time to time. Superstition too. I believe,' she whispered, 'that the coats are cursed. Now carefully zip up the bags, child, and come over here to me.'

At the steps Miss Firbanks slipped a yellow ribbon over Bridie's head and Bridie felt the cold touch of metal against her skin.

'What is it?' she asked.

'A master key,' replied Miss Firbanks. 'It will open any door at the Bazaar. I want you to have it. I have one, Branwell has his, and this one is yours . . . Now come, child, let us leave this dreary place.'

As she was turning the key in the lock of the understairs door, Miss Firbanks's head rose to listen. Bridie heard the sound too. A whistle—distant yet piercingly clear. No sooner had it died away than the same set of notes was taken up and whistled on by a second person, then by a third, then by others, until they heard it go over the Bazaar, jumping into the heart of the city. There it simply exploded, shooting in all directions like a sound firework: the air crisscrossed with shrill calls and answers and every dog at the Bazaar doing its utmost to drown them out.

Bare feet came slapping down the marble stairs. Branwell, half tucked in, half buttoned up, flew by, never noticing Miss Firbanks and Bridie standing in the shadows. The revolving doors spun madly as he dived out into the night. Seconds later they heard him join in with the whistling, repeating the same sequence of long and short notes. Like bird song.

He managed to keep it up for at least ten minutes. Returning inside, he was surprised to find Miss Firbanks and Bridie waiting for him.

'What is it, Branwell?' demanded Miss Firbanks. 'What is the news on the streets?'

Branwell hugged himself, grinning stupidly with happiness. 'Omar has come!' he cried. 'He is here in the city.'

'Who's Omar?' asked Bridie.

'Omar?' said Branwell looking at her with blank incomprehension. 'Why, Omar is the best man in the world. Some call him the king of the street people.'

He ran up to Bridie and seized her arm. 'And if Omar can't find out what's happened to your grandfather, then no man can.'

CHAPTER TEN

THE FOLLOWING DAY an unfamiliar smell wafted down the stairwell from the Bazaar's old cafeteria.

'Hey, that's wonderful!' cried Bridie sniffing long and hard. 'If I didn't know better I'd say someone was baking.'

'They are,' grinned Branwell. 'Or should I say *she* is?'

'But I thought—'

'It's a tradition. Miss Firbanks always bakes oatmeal cakes for Omar when he comes to the city. It's the only time she tries her hand at something other than her universal vegetable hash.' And he added, 'We'll take them tonight when we call at Soap Hill.'

Bridie felt nervous. 'Do you really think Omar'll be able to help us?'

Branwell shrugged. 'He will if he can. All we can do is wait and see.'

Then Miss Firbanks barged through the doors, her skirt, cardigan, and boots speckled with flour. Indeed she left a trail of flour in her wake. 'What, still gossiping?' she said testily. 'Come along—I can find plenty for you to do.'

Bridie was glad to be kept busy, otherwise she was sure the hours would drag. But her mind wasn't on what she was doing. When she broke Shah's favourite drinking bowl, Miss Firbanks shrieked, 'Child, I have no idea what's wrong with you today, but you're use to neither man nor beast!'

Bridie apologized profusely—as she did when she spilt the bird seed and left the tap running in the yard.

By mid afternoon it began to grow dark, the city's lights forming a glowing canopy over the distant roof-tops, and the headlights of the rush hour traffic crept between buildings. Slowly the moon edged up over the curry-paste Devil who suddenly flickered and, hey presto, was illuminated himself.

The night was well advanced when two figures stepped out of the Bazaar, both buttoned and muffled against the cold. Spider made three, of course, but he was tucked snugly into Branwell's overcoat, his head just showing beneath Branwell's chin. Hurrying over the waste ground, they reached the busy streets, becoming swept up in the flow.

As they went their mood was solemn. Branwell talked and Bridie listened; and Branwell's talk concerned mainly Omar who had last visited the city three years ago.

'He never stays in one place long,' explained Branwell. 'That's why a visit is so special.'

In Charles Street they noticed Snail loitering by a hole in the road, her eye obviously caught by the handsome black and white checked cones surrounding it. She shot Branwell and Bridie an indifferent glance.

'Ain't doing no 'arm,' she snapped defensively; then recognizing Bridie she mumbled, 'S'pose you goin' to ask about that grandad of yourn again?'

'No,' replied the girl breezily. 'Actually we're on our way to Omar, to ask him instead.'

'Aren't you going too, Snail?' enquired Branwell.

Snail sniffed, the dew-drop on the end of her nose danced. 'Might be. Might not. Might be takin' a present wiv me too.' She nodded at the cones. 'Might take one to 'im an' tell 'im to set it down where 'e pleases. Surprise move, see? Leads to int'resting developments.'

Clearly she was not about to be rushed into a quick decision on the matter, so they left her, shuffling along, bent double beneath her cardboard box, all her pans clanking like discordant wind chimes.

They crossed the iron bridge.

There appeared to be a great many more people encamped on Soap Hill than usual, to judge by the number of fires. In fact the whole hill was orange with firelight and shadows went curling up to the soap factory, which seemed even more like a besieged castle.

From under the railway viaduct, Bridie heard a fiddle; and two Salvation Army ladies were dancing together, swishing their skirts and laughing like young girls. Many Romanies were there too, trading briskly in ponies and horses, concluding each deal with a spit in the palm and a handshake; while elsewhere, crowding the fires, all manner of travellers, tricksters, drifters, and down-at-heels sat warming themselves and cooking their suppers.

Bridie was amazed. 'These people here because of Omar?' she asked.

Branwell nodded.

Someone shouted across to them and Selection Box and Spout Nose strolled over arm in arm.

'Do I smell oatmeal cakes?' asked Spout Nose sniffing the air.

Branwell held up an elaborately wrapped basket. 'Can't fool that nose of yours,' he grinned.

'We've been looking out for you,' said Selection Box. 'We knew you'd be here.'

'On account of your grandpa,' said Spout Nose. 'I mean Omar can work the streets like nobody else. He can get word across the city in a matter of days.'

'But they have to wait their turn, don't they, Spout Nose?'

'They most certainly do,' said Spout Nose, springing on his toes and sounding official. 'There's many who waits on Omar's time.' And leaning forward he whispered, 'He asked us—me and Selection Box here—to make sure there was some sort of order with those as waits. Right, take down their names, Selection Box.'

Selection Box produced a grubby piece of paper and

licked a stub of pencil. 'Names?' he demanded, his pencil hovering in readiness and his expression keenness itself.

'Come on, Selection Box, you know who I am,' said Branwell, wondering whether to be amused or offended.

Selection Box stared hard at him for failing to do things properly. Branwell sighed and obligingly spoke his name— spelling it out for him very slowly. Afterwards Bridie was forced to do the same.

Spout Nose said stiffly, 'If you would do us the honour of waiting here by the fire, we shall summon you when 'tis your turn.'

'But—' Bridie's mouth fell open in dismay. To no avail. Spout Nose and Selection Box had already hurried away, eager to add new names to their list.

Reluctantly she sat by the fire next to Branwell, around it were many friendly faces, and there were numerous diversions to watch. At any other time Bridie might have laughed and enjoyed herself. But not tonight. Slowly the moon crawled up in the sky and yet still more folk continued arriving at Soap Hill, all intent, it seemed, on an audience with the king of the street people.

Towards midnight, Spout Nose and Selection Box reappeared.

'*H*if you care to *h*a-ccompany *h*us,' said Selection Box, whose grand manner by now had run completely out of control. '*W*hee w*h*ill constrain you to the great man 'imself w*h*ith all due conglomeration.'

Bridie jumped up. 'At last! Come on, Branwell,' she cried, dragging him to his feet.

With Spout Nose in front and Selection Box behind, they were escorted to a huge fire close to the top of the hill. Many people sat there, but at that particular moment, Omar himself was hidden behind a wall of flames.

Then suddenly Bridie saw him, beaming across at her, holding out his hands in a gesture of welcome. On his wrists silver bracelets jangled and shone.

Omar was an elegant Ethiopian, his skin the darkest skin could be, his hair and beard peppered with grey. He sat draped in a blanket, a staff and pair of army boots by his side and his feet naked and veined.

He beckoned them closer, his long fingers showing a half moon on every nail.

'Brother—sister!' he boomed, and when Spider scrambled up his arm, he chuckled saying, 'And not forgetting little brother too.'

Gently he petted the monkey, lazily half closing his creamy blood-shot eyes. Bridie noticed how rarely he opened them, yet when he did it was shocking and unexpected—like a cat striking out with its claws.

Standing beside him, Bridie found herself lost for words.

Omar understood. He took her hand and drew her nearer; and she stared down at those wonderful long fingers.

'You have not been a street person for long, sister,' he said, his breath warm upon her.

Overcome as usual by curiosity, Bridie looked up and said, 'How can you be so sure?'

'Your nails betray you, sister. The city's grime has not yet made them black like those of our friends around us.'

'Black enough,' mused Bridie. 'Aunt Dolly would have a fit if she saw them.'

Omar laughed. A gentle mocking laugh—which is not to say unkind; and Bridie thought it was possible to love him for his laugh alone.

'Tell me about her,' he said.

So Bridie began to tell him, speaking as if he had commanded her. She started badly at first, tripping over her words, while all the time fearing she would stray from the point or make an utter gabbling fool of herself along the way. Soon, however, she found herself chatting to Omar as if they were the only two by the fire and had known each other for months rather than minutes. She told him everything, including how he might be able to help.

Omar listened intently, his fingers stroking Spider and his eyes half closed. When she finished, Bridie said 'Oh!' as if surprised to find herself there.

For a while Omar said nothing. Bridie thought he was waiting for her to go. Suddenly he turned to her, opening his eyes a fraction more.

'Sister,' he said softly. 'Your grandfather is unknown to me. Yet, from what you tell me, I am willing to believe him a good man. I will send word out on the streets through my people. When news reaches me, you shall hear. That is a promise.'

Bridie felt so happy she nearly hugged him there and then. Restraining herself she managed to thank him politely and Branwell set down the cakes his mother had baked.

'Ah, I knew Miss Firbanks would not forget me,' boomed Omar, his laugh rising from deep inside his chest.

As Branwell and Bridie were preparing to take their leave, Spider suddenly leapt upon Branwell's shoulders pacing backwards and forwards in an agitated manner, his fur bristling.

'What is it?' asked Bridie.

'There,' pointed Branwell and his mouth turned downwards.

Hovering on the edge of the firelight were the loathsome, cringing figures of the Crickbones.

'Oh, great Omar!' they sneered, seeming to bite off chunks of darkness and spit them out.

'King of gutters!'

'Lord of dustbins!'

'Prince of nothing!'

Omar widened his eyes, but his voice remained good natured. 'Brothers, you are welcome at my fire,' he called.

'Nobody welcomes the Crickbones,' snarled Amos. 'We are welcomed like a disease.'

'And look—look!' Deakin began shrieking. 'The *spy* is with him!'

'All plotting together.'

'Plotting against us.'

'Trying to rid the world of the Crickbone brothers.'

Branwell took a step forward. 'You best go now,' he said darkly.

'No,' said Omar. 'Let them stay if they wish.'

'We have no need to sit at your fire, Omar,' said the Crickbones slyly. 'We have a fire of our own and a house to go around it.'

'How can you say that?' shouted Bridie suddenly losing her temper. 'It isn't your house at all—it belongs to my grandfather!'

The Crickbones grinned crookedly at each other, slowly shrinking back into the darkness until they had vanished.

CHAPTER ELEVEN

IN THE NIGHT the rain came. Bridie awoke to the sound of it hammering against the boarded windows. For nearly a week it rained hard and persistently, slanting down from sluggish grey clouds that hung over the city and obscured the tops of the high-rise offices.

The Bazaar sprang more leaks than an old tramp steamer. Water splattered upon the marble stairway, trickled down the steps and made ponds of the landings. Buckets and bowls were commandeered from the hardware department, but perversely, for every leak caught, a new one appeared somewhere else.

The damp worked its way into people, as well as buildings. Branwell was moody and Miss Firbanks had a permanently foul temper. On a whim she decided to hold an economy drive. They were burning too many candles, she announced, and that was a perfect waste of good money. In a self-sacrificing example she adjusted her hurricane lamp to its lowest flame and stalked the Bazaar extinguishing all the lights she considered unnecessary—which meant all the lights she found. Soon it was depressingly gloomy as well as damp. And Branwell and Bridie put on second coats when Miss Firbanks began turning down paraffin heaters too.

It was almost a blessed relief to be outside, but even at Soap Hill a dispiriting cloud hovered. Beneath the viaduct's arches, wet fires guttered and street people sat huddled in sheets of plastic. Amongst their numbers must have been Omar, but Bridie and Branwell caught no further sight of him there.

Bridie grew increasingly fretful with the passing of days.

'What if he forgets?' she said.

'Omar won't forget,' said Branwell.

'He might.'

'Other men might—not Omar.'

It was midday when they heard the whistles start up again.

They were in Angel Street: Bridie was struggling to carry a number of rolled-up posters and kept dropping them; Branwell had a bucket of paste and a paste brush, which Spider jealously took against as if it were another creature. The posters were a tirade against people's cruelty to animals. But they kept peeling off the walls. Branwell accused Bridie of not mixing the paste strong enough; and when at last he managed to get some to stay up, Bridie told him they were crooked.

'They're not supposed to be works of art,' said Branwell sullenly.

Then the whistles began. Not shrill and joyful this time—but long, melancholic notes. Branwell glanced anxiously at Bridie and, putting his fingers to his tongue, sent the message a few more streets along.

When he stopped, Bridie said accusingly, 'It's about Omar—he's leaving, isn't he?'

Branwell nodded.

'But you told me—'

'Come on, if we hurry we might just catch him at Soap Hill.'

They dropped everything they were carrying and ran, their feet splashing through puddles and Spider clinging unhappily to Branwell's back. In the air the whistles still flew by, but the intervals of silence were growing longer. Just over the iron bridge they found Selection Box and Spout Nose sitting by a fire.

'Where's Omar?' panted Bridie at once.

'Omar?' said Spout Nose blinking up from the flames

where a billycan was fast coming to the boil. 'Why Omar's gone. Didn't you hear the whistles? He's fresh away on his travels.'

Sensing something was wrong, Selection Box said, 'Stay for a brew-up, why don't you? These leaves have been boiled but the once, there's plenty more flavour left in 'em.'

'No . . . No thanks,' muttered Bridie.

She turned and marched away. Branwell glanced helplessly at Spout Nose and Selection Box and ran after her, catching her at the iron bridge, where she leaned over the parapet staring blankly into the water. The moment Branwell touched her all her disappointment turned to anger.

'You said! You promised!' she shouted. 'You told me Omar wouldn't forget!'

No words of Branwell's could excuse him or console her, and a dreadful silence lay between them as they slowly returned to the Bazaar.

After days of relentless rain, the waste ground surrounding the old department store had practically turned into a mire. Bridie, half blinded by tears, slid and floundered. Then her boots got stuck. She fought for balance, lost it, fell slowly backwards and landed unceremoniously in the mud.

She let out a scream of frustration, beating the ground with her fist.

'Sister,' called a booming, half-amused voice. 'You look in need of a helping hand.'

Bridie quickly blinked away her tears. 'Omar?'

Sure enough, Omar stepped out from the Bazaar's doorway and came striding straight towards her, his great boots slurping through the mud, his staff steadying him like a ship's rudder. Despite the frayed piece of tarpaulin that cloaked his back, he looked every inch a king. Reaching Bridie he gently lifted her to her feet and stood resting his forehead against his staff, his eyes half closed as if dozing.

'I can't believe it,' murmured Bridie. 'You really came.'

'Didn't I give my word?' said Omar.

'Have you heard something?' she begged. 'Some news about Gramps? Please tell me!'

Gently Omar tilted her chin to meet his gaze. 'Yes, sister, I bring news,' he said. 'Word has come back from the streets. Your grandfather is well.'

'But where? . . . How—?'

'Come. I will take you to where you can find him. You must ask your own questions there.' And he would say no more on the matter, only smiling when Bridie pressed him.

They immediately set off, Omar refusing to be hurried, despite Bridie's understandable impatience, and on reaching the streets he led the way with his staff, forcing the traffic to a halt before him.

''Ere! Who do you think you are?' shouted an angry lorry driver. 'The Prince of Wales?'

Omar smiled. Why, anyone could see that he was more than a prince. Strolling down the crowded pavements, people naturally stood aside for him; and, if some also stopped to stare, Omar didn't mind. In fact he never even noticed. The city was as good as invisible to him. In his mind he was crossing the wide, open plains of Africa.

'Where do you think he's taking us?' whispered Bridie, who, with Branwell, followed behind like Omar's attendants.

'Who can say?' shrugged Branwell.

Then Omar turned away from the busy main streets.

'I know this place!' cried Bridie, her memory jogged by a passing train. They were in the alley behind the old nail factory, although it appeared very different by daylight. She saw Omar stop and beam at her.

'I am informed you have been here before, sister,' he said.

'Yes, but how—'

'You were not to know, but that night you were very close to your grandfather.' Omar paused then added, 'Make your way down on to the tracks again, but this time keep the tunnel behind you. Go on until you come to a siding. It will seem overgrown and unused. Look here for your grandfather. His home is an old railway carriage.'

Bridie tried to imagine the scene, but found she couldn't.

Suddenly Omar pulled the tarpaulin close about him.

Bridie stared. 'But you're not going?' she cried in dismay. 'You can't—not now—we still need you!'

For a moment it appeared as if Omar was going to speak sharply to her. Instead he murmured, 'I have my own road to go, sister.'

'And the Crickbones?' asked Branwell. 'Are we likely to run into Amos and Deakin?'

Omar smiled saying, 'At present our *friends* are occupied with more pressing business—of which, no doubt, you will learn soon enough. No, you will not cross paths with brother Amos and brother Deakin, have no fears of that.'

He rested his hands on Bridie's shoulders. 'Wait no longer, sister,' he urged. 'Your grandfather has much need of you.'

He smiled once more then turned and unhurriedly began to walk away.

'Goodbye, Omar!' Bridie was madly shouting. 'And thank you. Thank you so much!'

Omar walked on; Branwell, Bridie, and Spider now as unreal to him as the rest of the city.

'Come on,' said Branwell tugging Bridie's arm. 'I should like to meet this grandfather of yours.'

Chapter Twelve

THE CLIMB DOWN the embankment to the railway line proved no easier having the benefit of full daylight. Every step was treacherously slippy and the thorns had lost none of their sharpness.

However, with just a few scratches to show for their troubles, they eventually emerged on to the open line. Seeing the tunnel, Bridie shuddered and turned her back on it, following Branwell along the shiny track—going in single file, because the space between the track and embankment was narrow and they had to be prepared in case a train came by. But, as luck would have it, none did and they were spared the indignity of having to throw themselves into the brambles.

They had been walking only a few minutes when Branwell pointed and said, 'Look, Bridie—a set of points. That must be for the siding Omar was telling us about.'

Branwell was right. Veering off the main track, seemingly into the embankment itself, curved a second set of rails. They were brown with rust and probably unused in years.

This was confirmed when they reached the entrance to the siding itself. So overgrown was it that anyone speeding by in a train would not realize it was there at all. The siding was like a secret valley: saplings and stunted bushes had sprung up between the rotten sleepers, with other vegetation growing out from its sides, forming a canopy overhead. In the summertime, with the trees in leaf, it must have been more dark and gloomy than it was at present.

Suddenly Bridie found she couldn't take another step.

'What is it?' asked Branwell, staring at her.

'Oh, Branwell,' she said. 'I'm afraid.'

'Of what? Your own grandfather?'

'But he might have changed.'

'And he might not,' said Branwell firmly. 'Come on, Bridie, I promise you'll not face him alone.'

They entered the siding like explorers, thrashing back branches that swept low into their faces. But soon the biggest obstacle became the rubbish littering the ground, the rusting barrels and spools of wire, the broken bottles and dustbin bags full and splitting.

Then the railway carriage came into view.

It lay at the end of the line, pressed up against the buffers, its maroon livery badly flaked and sides thick with ivy. The moment Bridie saw it, her eyes searched for some small detail she could associate with Gramps, but she saw nothing to reassure her, only what was derelict and abandoned.

Yet as they stood gazing at it, a figure came round the side carrying a bucket. He was a tired old man in a grubby collar-less shirt and crumpled trousers. His sleeves were rolled up and his braces hung loose at his sides.

'Gramps!'

Bridie squeezed out the broken sound. Then she was madly shouting it. 'Gramps! Gramps!'

Startled, Mr Summers dropped the bucket, spilling corn seed on the ground. He got down with a groan, laboriously picking it up a seed at a time.

'Gramps—it's me!' cried Bridie hovering helplessly over him. 'Please . . . look up and see.'

'Must pick every bit up,' fretted the old man. 'Must pick it up or Mr Amos and Mr Deakin will be angry. They mustn't find out how clumsy I've been.'

Bridie didn't know what to do. She turned to Branwell who stood with Spider a little further off. He saw how confused she looked and made a pushing motion with his hands, signalling don't give up. Blinking back her tears, Bridie sank down and helped pick up the spilt corn.

'Must get it back into the bucket,' the old man told her. 'If they find out, I shall be in hot water again.'

After a few minutes they had done the best they could and Bridie helped carry the bucket to the carriage.

An orange-box made a step up to the door. Inside a dim corridor ran the carriage's length, which was otherwise divided into three compartments. Mr Summers shuffled to an end compartment and slid open the door. Bridie followed him through.

This, she saw, was the limit of her grandfather's living quarters, the only barely inhabitable space in the carriage: one of the seats being made up into a bed and a string luggage-rack containing the old man's precious few belongings.

Despite the 'no smoking' sign on the window, an old oil heater was doing precisely that, without throwing out much in the way of heat to dry a line of socks that Bridie had to duck to avoid. Mildew spotted the ceiling and ivy grew through the window. Altogether it was gloomy and damp and reeked of oil and rotting wood.

Mr Summers sat down on his bed, his shoulders rounded and his hands clasping his knees. After a while he looked up at Bridie as if for the first time and a faint glimmer of recognition came into his eyes.

'I once knew a girl,' he said softly. 'Looked just like you . . . my granddaughter Bridie.'

Bridie placed her hands over her grandfather's hands, feeling how cold and gnarled they were.

'Gramps, it *is* me,' she said. 'It's me—Bridie.' She smiled with relief. He must have mistaken me for a boy, she thought, because of my clothes.

She lay her head against his shoulder. 'Oh, Gramps, I've been searching such a long time to find you.'

The old man sniffed and thrust up his spectacles, wiping his moist eyes with a finger and thumb. He blinked around him. 'There's nothing I can give you,' he said. 'I wish I knew you were coming . . . I do . . . I . . . I'm not used to company you see . . . There's nothing to give you.'

'It doesn't matter,' said Bridie squeezing his hand. 'I came to see you.'

Neither of them spoke for a long time. Then Bridie said, 'What are you doing here, Gramps? Was it the Crickbones? Did they cheat you out of your yard? Is that how it happened?'

Mr Summers took out a yellow handkerchief, wiped his nose, then began to speak.

'It's not that I ever much cared for either of them,' he said. 'But I used to feel sorry for them. I'd give them money when they brought things for my yard, you know, slip 'em a little bit extra. But recently business's been bad. Really bad. For the first time in my life, Bridie, I'm ashamed to say I owed money. Somehow the Crickbones got to hear of it. They said they wanted to help me—for past kindnesses or so they claimed—and they spoke of lending me as much money as I needed to tide me over. I must admit I was surprised to hear they had anything more than a few pennies to their name and like a fool I believed them. I suppose I was swept along by it all. I . . . ended signing an agreement I never ought to have signed.'

He dabbed his eyes.

'Do you know where the Crickbones got the money from?' asked Bridie.

Mr Summers shook his head.

'What happened next?'

'Oh, it started getting bad,' said Mr Summers. 'Suddenly the brothers were demanding repayments. I seemed to owe more and more each week, and I couldn't do anything about it because I had signed their agreement, so everything was above board and legal. Eventually they squeezed my last penny out of me. I had nothing left to give them but my yard. Funny, but thinking back, I now see this was what they wanted all along.'

'Poor old Gramps,' said Bridie hugging him.

At that moment, Spider innocently sauntered in and sat watching them.

Bridie felt a jolt go through her grandfather.

'A cat!' she heard him utter.

Suddenly he was struggling to his feet, shouting, 'A cat! Who let a cat in here? Don't they know what trouble they'll land me in?'

Before Bridie could prevent him, Mr Summers snatched up a broom and took a swing at Spider, who quickly somersaulted to safety. The broom struck a tea pot and it smashed to the floor, spilling old leaves and cold tea.

'But, Gramps!' cried Bridie. 'It's only Spider—Spider's not a cat!'

'They say I have to keep cats away!' shouted Mr Summers. 'All cats! Every cat!'

Nimbly Spider leapt on to the string luggage rack as Mr Summers swung out with the broom again. He hit the luggage rack and it rained boxes and tins upon him.

Spider unhurt—except for his feelings—jumped clear of the broom and went streaking from the compartment.

Mr Summers stumbled and collapsed on to the bed. He sat running his fingers through his hair.

'That's what they tell me to do,' he groaned. 'I have to keep cats away at all costs.'

'Away from what, Gramps?' asked Bridie.

Before the old man could answer, Branwell came racing in. The whole carriage rocked and his face was black with anger. In his arms he cradled the unhappy monkey.

'What happened?' he demanded. 'What frightened Spider?'

Suspiciously he eyed the broom still clutched by Mr Summers and reached his own conclusions.

'Branwell, you have to understand—' began Bridie.

'If you would be so good as to come with me, Mr

Summers,' said Branwell tight-lipped. 'I think you've got some explaining to do.'

'Branwell!' exclaimed Bridie, shocked to hear him address the old man in such a brisk way, but Branwell turned and marched off.

Outside he stood waiting for them, stonily watching on, as Bridie helped her grandfather to the ground. Without any further explanation, he led the way round to the back of the carriage.

There, haphazardly set out, Bridie saw a number of small caged enclosures which she recognized at once.

'Gramps!' she cried delightedly. 'You still keep chickens.'

Attracted by her voice, several brightly coloured cockerels stepped out of their boxes to investigate. They were proud, strutting creatures with elegant drooping tails, the sheen on their feathers handsomely metallic.

Recognizing Mr Summers, the birds ran towards him. He opened a hatch and lifted one out, cooing and clucking at it and smoothing down its feathers.

'Is that right, Mr Summers?' asked Branwell coldly. 'Are these birds yours?'

'No,' answered Mr Summers good-naturedly. 'These beauties belong to Amos and Deakin. They allow me to stay here as long as I take care of them. See, son, they know me to be quite knowledgeable about chickens. Used to keep birds of my own. You ask Bridie, there's nothing I'm more fonder of than a freshly laid egg.'

'Well, you can't claim these birds are good layers,' said Branwell sarcastically. 'I mean there isn't a single hen amongst them. They're all males, Mr Summers. Cockerels.'

'That's right,' said Mr Summers. 'Show birds. I believe the brothers enter them for competitions.'

Branwell sneered, 'These are not show birds, Mr Summers. These are fighting birds—bred to fight to the death.'

Bridie glared at him. Was he suggesting her grandfather

could be involved in something so illegal and barbaric as cock fighting?

'How can you be so sure?' she demanded.

Branwell took the bird from Mr Summers, handling it as expertly as the old man had, so it could not struggle or flap its wings. He turned it until they could see its legs.

'Look,' he said. 'It's had its spurs cut off. All the birds have.'

Bridie knew enough about chickens to know the spur extended from the back of the claw, and when male birds fought it was used like a knife—but rarely was deadly. She was puzzled. Without spurs there was even less chance of a bird hurting its rival than usual.

'A metal spur is tied on in its place,' said Branwell, his eyes dark and angry. 'That way the birds do terrible damage to each other.'

Old Mr Summers looked perplexed. 'But it's in the birds' blood to fight, son. You can't breed that out of them. The males fight each other for territory and females.'

'But not to the death,' said Branwell savagely. 'Not for *entertainment*.'

'It's not Gramps's fault,' said Bridie leaping to her grandfather's defence. 'He wasn't to know.'

'Then he should have guessed,' said Branwell. 'Those Crickbones will do anything to get their filthy hands on easy money. Listen, old man, why do you think the birds are kept here in secret—away from prying eyes?' He shook his head. 'There are some'll pay big money to watch cruelty to animals. Sick people who call it sport!'

'But I wouldn't get involved in such a thing,' protested Mr Summers. 'Look at the beautiful plumage. I wouldn't hurt these birds for the world. Tell me how, son, and I'll put matters to rights straight away.'

'We need to act quickly,' said Branwell pacing up and down. 'We have to get the birds away from here before the Crickbones return—'

'You're too late, son,' said Mr Summers. 'They came and took most of the birds first thing this morning. Said they wanted to prepare them for a *big show* tonight.'

'Then it's too late,' cried Branwell bitterly. 'There's nothing we can do.'

'Not unless we go to Gramps's yard and rescue them there,' said Bridie.

Branwell shook his head. 'Impossible. They'll probably have look-outs posted, watching for the law. We'd be spotted a mile off.'

But Bridie had an idea.

'We could always go through the scrapyard,' she said. 'It joins right on to Gramps's.'

Branwell was unenthusiastic. 'That place is worse than a jungle, we'll never get through it. Besides, it could be dangerous at night.'

'Not if we have a guide.'

'Who?'

'What about Spout Nose?' she suggested.

'Of course,' said Branwell. 'He lives in the scrapyard. He shares the top of an old double decker bus with Selection Box.'

Branwell paused, thoughtfully weighing up the possibilities of Bridie's plan. Deciding it was worth a try he suddenly became animated.

'Right, you lot, there's not a moment to lose. Let's get these remaining birds rounded up and taken to the Bazaar.' And to himself he said, 'Then there's a little favour I must ask of a friend of mine up on Soap Hill.'

CHAPTER THIRTEEN

THAT NIGHT THE fires on Soap Hill were banked extra high against the cold.

Branwell studied the clouded sky with approval. 'At least there's no moon,' he noted.

Spout Nose sniffed. 'But I can smell snow, Branwell,' he said, adding wistfully, 'Perhaps we should think of calling off our little adventure until the weather promises better.'

'Spout Nose!' said Branwell reproachfully. 'We need you to guide us through the scrapyard and you promised you would.'

'I know—I know,' said Spout Nose unhappily. 'But why me? Why not Selection Box. He knows the scrapyard as well as I do.'

'Because with that nose of yours you can smell out trouble like you can smell out changes in the weather,' replied Branwell.

Bridie stood nearby feeling nervous. She wondered if the others felt quite as nervous as she did. She clutched her grandfather's hand. He had insisted on coming as far as Soap Hill. Beyond that the scrapyard would prove too much of an ordeal for him. He would have to stay behind with Selection Box and anxiously await their return.

Time came to say their goodbyes. Then Branwell, Spout Nose, Bridie, and Spider took their leave, Branwell leading them down Soap Hill. On his back he carried a rucksack (acquired from the camping department, of course); and Bridie also noticed a catapult in his jeans pocket, its new elastic swinging loose like a tail.

'I can't say I likes this one little bit,' whispered Spout

Nose. 'There's too much danger involved for my liking.'

Bridie smiled and patted his arm. How could she tell him she felt exactly the same?

'Come on! Don't lag behind,' they heard Branwell call.

The curry-paste Devil was waiting for them on the corner. It was so cold they were able to blow back their own breath at him. Unimpressed, the Devil showed them how to make a proper smoke ring—which he never tired of doing in the cause of Poona curry paste. Then they turned under an arch and entered a cobweb of mean twisting alleys.

Suddenly, a car—its engine purring and headlights pearly white—came crawling around a corner, catching them unaware.

'In here,' whispered Branwell shoving his companions down into a doorway like a bundle of rags. The big black car crept by without stopping, rolling slightly on the potholes. Branwell stood up, scanning the alley after it. The spectators were arriving and time was running short.

They hurried on, skirting the scrapyard's boundary until Spout Nose said, 'This is the place, Branwell.'

He pushed against the corrugated fence and a narrow section opened as neatly as a door. Silently they filed through the gap.

As dark and poorly lit as the alley had been, Bridie was quite unprepared for the pitch blackness lying in wait for her. It was like a wall. She gasped as she struck it. Reaching out a hand she touched something soft and slightly sticky. It was a rubber tyre.

A thousand old, worn tyres were stacked up before her like the defences of a massive grim fortress. Now that her eyes were accustomed to the new level of darkness, she tilted back her head to stare up at it. The regularly placed tyres created an impression of being woven, rather than built. The wall seemed to ripple and sway. Surely it would come crashing down at any moment? But even as she watched, it slowly grew less insubstantial, resuming its previous, formidable bulk.

Branwell pushed her on. 'Don't lose sight of Spout Nose,' he warned.

Like a real fortress, the fortress of tyres was not without its passageways and dark stifling tunnels. Nothing was straight when it might follow a corkscrew path; and lesser passageways were constantly striking off upon either side. It would have been impossible finding a way through without Spout Nose as their guide. He told Bridie that he and Selection Box had built several bolt-holes here. Street people need to have at least one secret place to hide.

Then Branwell shushed him quiet and they pressed on in silence.

By now the tyres had lost their towers and turrets and become cliffs and canyons. It was hot, dirty work getting through them, and in the dark only Spider moved with any degree of sure footedness.

At last they reached a wide clearing. They should have felt better for having left the oppressive tyre dump behind, but Spout Nose's nostrils began twitching, making him edgy and suggesting unknown dangers lurked close by.

Branwell crouched down. Bridie noticed him slip off his rucksack and take something from it, but it was too small to make out, even when he loaded it into his catapult ready for firing.

Still crouching he gave a soft whistle.

That same moment the darkness violently stirred and something large and terrifying came bounding towards them. Bridie saw its fangs and was unable to move. Spider streaked up her as if she were a pole. Then the savage barking began.

The guard dog was as big and fierce as a wolf. It hurled itself directly at Branwell, strings of saliva trailing from its jaws. And just when it seemed nothing could stop it falling upon him and tearing him flesh from bone, the wire to its collar went taut. With a yelp, the dog was yanked backwards, sprawling in the dust, panting and whimpering.

Branwell fired his catapult.

His shot, not intended to hurt or even hit the dog, dropped beside it. Suspicious, then curious, the dog stood up, sniffed it and swallowed it down in a single gulp. Meantime Branwell had reloaded his catapult. He stretched back the elastic and fired a second piece of meat, which was similarly devoured, this time without the precautionary sniff.

Two more pieces were required before the dog yawned, laid its head on its paws and fell into a deep, drugged sleep.

Cautiously Branwell led the others to its side. They gathered round watching its chest rhythmically rise and fall. Spider, overcoming his fears, climbed down beside Bridie as she ran her fingers through the thick, coarse fur.

Branwell told them it would wake in a few hours and be none the worse for its sleep.

'It wouldn't be so bad if this were the only one,' said Spout Nose, nervously glancing around. 'We best stay on our guard against others.'

For the time being, Branwell stuffed his catapult into his back pocket.

Hearing the murmur of voices, Bridie stood up and glanced across at the opposite side of the clearing. She saw two motionless cranes rising above a graveyard of cars, the cars' glassless hulks stacked one on top of another, five sometimes six vehicles high. On dented chrome-work light glittered. But not starlight.

Chapter Fourteen

Despite Bridie's misgivings, the wall of stacked cars turned out to be by no means as dense and impenetrable as the tyre fortress: many cars, robbed of doors and seats, were little more than metal shells, with tangles of wires left hanging where dashboards had been.

If care was taken to avoid broken glass (which sparkled everywhere in nuggets like diamonds) it was an easy matter to work through one vehicle to the next. In such a way, Spout Nose led Branwell, Bridie, and Spider to the far side of the wall.

There, crowding around the glassless windscreen of a car wreck, they peered out. An unobstructed view of Mr Summers's yard presented itself, and Bridie was glad her grandfather wasn't there to see it for himself—it would have broken his heart.

The wreckers' yard made its own wall and boundary on three sides of Mr Summers's property, while the gate and fence along Rivet Lane occupied the fourth side. The house stood in darkness and a ring of straw bales before it marked out a fighting pit.

Dotted around the ring stood men idly talking in low voices, some smoking fat cigars, some drinking champagne, swigging it down straight from the bottle. They wore formal suits, every last man of them, the more extrovert favouring winged collars, bow ties, and purple cummerbunds. Clearly, however, they were not comfortable to be so stiffly dressed. They fingered their collars, pulled at their cuffs and worked their shoulders inside the tight confines of their jackets.

'What a gallery of rogues,' whispered Spout Nose. 'Although I bet their own mothers wouldn't recognize 'em tonight, done up in them fancy hired suits.'

'You know these men?' asked Bridie astonished.

'I'd say—but I'd rather cross the street than meet any one of them face to face. It's Beau Scriven's gang. Amos and Deakin are swimming with sharks if they are fallen in with him. In fact it's a black day for us all if Scriven's moving into the area.'

Apart from the men, there was also a small number of women. They were bored, bloodless creatures shivering in skimpy sequinned dresses and loathing every second spent at the yard. Now and again the men would erupt into laughter, drawing the women's tight, scowling faces across at them, but never were they permitted to share the joke.

'And look over there,' said Bridie.

Like a pair of shifty polecats, Amos and Deakin could be seen skulking between the different parties, abused by the men, icily ignored by the women. Yet beneath the cover of greasy smiles, fawning looks, and unctuous words, the Crickbones craftily collected the half empty bottles of champagne and discarded cigar butts, concealing them in an old battered pram. Whenever a particularly rich picking chanced their way, the brothers exchanged smug, knowing looks and grinned.

So much was possible to observe because fires burning in oil drums gave out a steady if smoky light, while the working headlights in the wall of scrap cars were also put to good purpose: their beams, in pairs or singular, crooked and crisscrossing, were much less reliable and occasionally, as a battery died, so too did a particular set of headlights, its watery beams slowly fading away.

Suddenly Branwell tapped Bridie's shoulder and urgently pointed. Stacked by the side of Mr Summers's house stood a number of wicker baskets. 'That must be them,' he whispered. 'We have to get closer.'

They were about to move away when some five or six men burst noisily on to the scene, brandishing air rifles.

'Did you bag anything, Marco?' somebody called.

'You kidding?' replied Marco leaning his gun across his shoulder. 'Whole place is teeming with vermin.' And to illustrate his point, he held up his fist. Five large rats hung by their tails. The women shuddered in horror.

Serves them right, thought Bridie: of course the rats thrive, the Crickbones got rid of her grandfather's cats.

Marco grinned and shook the dead rats at Amos and Deakin saying, 'You disgusting Crickbones—you ought to carry a health warning.'

'How right you are, sir,' oozed Deakin, bowing and taking a crafty draw on a cigar, before passing it on to Amos.

'We are both so utterly loathsome,' added Amos winking back at his brother.

'Can't we start soon?' called one of the women sulkily. She shifted uncomfortably in her high-heeled shoes. 'This place gives me the creeps.'

The other women agreed and the men laughed indulgently as if at children. 'Start?' they said. 'How can we start? Boss hasn't arrived. Can't start without the boss.'

Marco said, 'But that's why we came back. His car's just pulled up.'

Bridie, as she crept after Branwell from one gutted car to the next, clearly heard every word that was spoken. She heard too the buzz of excitement that now greeted Marco's announcement. She couldn't resist lifting her head to take a look. Coming into the light, she saw a small man with a camel-hair coat draped over his shoulders. His smile was assured and unwavering, and his eyes flickered from face to face, as if taking into account who was present.

Immediately the men rushed to attend him like some great lord.

'Evening, Mr Scriven.'

'Glad to see you, Mr Scriven.'

'Looking good, Mr Scriven.'

Beau Scriven smiled slyly.

'Come on, Bridie,' whispered Branwell. 'We're nearly there.'

With a sigh Bridie lowered her head and the uncomfortable business of crawling through the wrecks went on a little longer.

Meanwhile Beau Scriven was addressing his followers. He was helped on to a straw bale and stood kid gloves in hand. 'My dear fellow villains,' he commenced, holding out his arms as if embracing them all and receiving a rousing cheer in return.

Hidden from view in the car stacks, Branwell at last halted.

'It's the nearest we can get to the house,' he told Bridie and Spout Nose. 'Unless we break cover, of course—but we'd be spotted as soon as we did.'

'So what do we do?' asked Bridie desperately.

Branwell reached over his shoulder and gently plucked Spider off his back, cradling the monkey's face close to his own.

'It's up to you now, Spider,' he murmured, stroking the creature's soft grey fur with his thumbs. 'If you can still remember what it's like to be locked up in a cage, you will do your best.'

Spider gave the boy a long wistful look, then struggled free and bounded away.

Bridie saw him streak across the open ground into the shadow of the house, straight away clambering to the top of the wicker baskets. She found she was holding her breath. Now came the difficult part as Spider tried to grip the peg securing the topmost door. But whichever way he tried, his small paws were not adapted for such a task. Instinctively he bit the peg instead, trusting more to the grip of his teeth than that of his fingers. But the peg refused to budge.

'Come on, Spider—you can do it,' willed Branwell.

Spider tried again with his paws—tugging and tugging until the whole stack of baskets swayed and was dangerously close to toppling over.

All at once the peg shot free and Spider flew backwards, falling to the ground with a somersault that couldn't have been neater if deliberately planned. Yet hardly was he down before he was leaping up again, eager to tackle the next pegged door.

'Look at him go!' laughed Branwell. 'See, he's worked out how to use his tail as an anchor. The genius! At this rate he'll have them all done in no time.'

This was just as well: Beau Scriven's speech was rapidly drawing to an end. It had been a long boastful speech, predicting great success in this, his latest criminal venture.

' . . . So let me thank you one and all for coming,' he was telling his crew and cronies. 'Tonight you shall be the first privileged few to witness the revival of part of our long-neglected sporting heritage. Enjoy it, my friends. After all, gentlemen of the underworld have always relished a certain amount of *freshly spilt blood.*'

The gang responded like dogs—baying. The noise was just what was required at that moment. Startled, the reluctant cockerels burst one by one from their baskets and finding themselves in dangerous open territory dived straight for cover. Within seconds they had dispersed under the derelict cars.

'Hurry, Spider—hurry!' urged Branwell as Spider set about freeing the last imprisoned bird.

The gang's approving roar was still in the air, when one of its members, who had drunk far too much champagne, jumped up on to the bales and draped his arm around Scriven in a familiar way he never would if sober. He raised an unsteady bottle. 'Whada-bout free cheers fa Beau?' he demanded. 'H-ip-Hip—!'

Then the drunk noticed Spider.

'Bli-mey!' he cried with genuine astonishment. 'Look art the size o' th-at rat!'

Unaware of the gathering danger, Spider released the last bird and was dancing triumphantly on top of the empty baskets.

He made a perfect target.

Something cracked.

Spider dropped to the ground.

Beau Scriven smiled and thrust back the gun to Marco.

CHAPTER FIFTEEN

A STORM OF rage and noise broke over the yard.

Men came pounding up, swearing and furiously beating the hollow cars like drums.

Women, convinced of the giant rat conspiracy, shrieked, one setting off another like alarms.

The cockerels were everywhere. Getting in the way. Flying up in a flurry of feathers. Squawking at their own shadows.

Bridie sat trembling. All she wanted to do was curl up with her hands pressed over her ears so she didn't have to hear the ugly threats that stabbed the air.

So much had happened so quickly. Skidding out of control. Like a car crash. Like the wrecks surrounding her. The moment Spider was shot, Branwell had gone a little insane. He broke cover, raced across to the wicker baskets and scooped up Spider's limp body, holding it in his arms like a rag doll.

'Murderers!' he roared, before diving back into the cars further up behind the house.

Without him Spout Nose panicked. 'We better get out of here,' he told Bridie, his face grey and gaunt with fear. But in the confusion, Bridie had lost him too and now she was all alone.

Calm at the centre of the storm stood Beau Scriven, the smile frozen to his face. The men were more fearful of him with that smile than if he had acted as crazy as they did.

'Who has done this?' he demanded, measuring out each terrible word. 'Who has dared to do this to Beau Scriven?'

All the men turned to Marco. He swallowed nervously. 'I

bet it was one of those tramps from up on Soap Hill, boss,' he said when something was needed to fill the waiting silence. 'I bet that's what it was. Some dirty tramp after a quick chicken supper.'

To Marco's surprise the cloud lifted from Scriven's face. He called his gang to him and they came running. Some had loosened their ties and undone top buttons. Some had dirt on their knees.

'Boys,' said Scriven, 'I promised you an evening of excitement—I promised you blood, and I don't mean to disappoint you now. If we can't have our sport one way, then we'll take it another. I say let's hunt down the filthy guttersnipe who thought he could put one over on Beau Scriven. Let's hunt him to ground and teach him a lesson he'll remember all his days—however short they may be.'

Bridie heard Scriven's chilling words and knew she had to get away—but which way was that? The heaped-up cars made a labyrinth in every direction she turned. She decided to play safe instead. She was thinking like a street person. It is always best to hide, they will tell you.

At the bottom of the car heap she discovered an old black taxi cab which, unlike so many of the other wrecks, had managed to retain its glass windows and seats. Squeezing through the door, she locked herself in, crouched down in the driver's seat, clutching the steering wheel, ready to speed away if only she could.

Thickly the silence gathered around her, growing in its own way as unsettling as the previous furore. Unable to sit still she was constantly turning to peer out of the windows, fearful in case something was there, but even more fearful if she did not look. She jumped at imagined sounds, her heart racing at shadows.

Suddenly the cab lurched violently and she was screaming.

Savagery was at the windscreen. Burrowing to get in. Claws skidding. A mass of bristling fur. Eyes burning.

Bridie's hand struck out, screams ripping from her in an unbroken string. She must have knocked a switch, for the windscreen-wipers jerked into life, smearing the dog's drool across the glass.

The dog fled at once.

With her head slumped upon the steering wheel, Bridie became lost in uncontrollable sobs, unable to stop herself and only gradually becoming aware of a familiar, friendly sound. She lifted her wet face, trying to catch her breath which still caught in her throat. The windscreen wipers were drily grinding back and forth—squealing to be shut off. Above them the sound of whistling arose a second time. It came from within the scrapyard itself and could only mean one thing—the street people were rallying to their aid!

Choking back her happiness Bridie wound down the window. The whistling immediately became louder, but more faintly came other sounds too. Sounds that by degrees grew more complex and distorted. It was a battle. Not with explosions and gun shots—it was far more primitive. Voices screamed and metal clashed against metal.

With the little that remained of her courage, Bridie wrenched open the cab's door and slipped out, crawling as fast as she could, until at last coming to the no man's land that set apart the wreckers' yard from the tyre dump.

The heart of the battle lay here as the tribe from Soap Hill pitted itself against Beau Scriven's robber barons, with lesser skirmishes breaking out along the dark walls of the tyre fortress, which were patrolled and stormed in various places, tyres bouncing down to repel the besiegers.

Somebody spoke Bridie's name.

She spun round.

'Spout Nose!' she gasped and all her strength left her.

Spout Nose ran forward, catching her just in time.

'I'll get you away from here, Miss Bridie,' he promised. 'This isn't the place for you.'

'But Branwell . . . '

'Branwell can take care of himself,' said Spout Nose firmly.

Bridie didn't resist and allowed herself to be led away around the edge of the battle into the silence of the tyre dump, whose narrow, confined ways were now oddly comforting.

'Look, Spout Nose!' said Bridie pointing up.

'What is it?' Spout Nose's expression turned distinctly worried.

'It's beginning to snow,' she said.

'Is that all,' said Spout Nose letting out his breath. 'I told you it would.'

They went on, occasionally challenged by a look-out posted high above them on the tyre walls, but without seeing another soul until they reached Soap Hill.

Then Gramps came hobbling up, holding out a blanket like a bull fighter, fussing around Bridie with it.

'For goodness' sake!' snapped Miss Firbanks, who was there too. 'Get the poor child to the fire and let her warm herself.'

Miss Firbanks, in her khaki army coat, must have rushed out in a great haste, snatching a hat off a mannequin on the way, but failing to notice the price tag hanging down at the back. Bridie thought how small and less formidable she looked outside the Bazaar. A batty old woman in a silly flowered hat.

As Bridie sat by the fire, Mr Summers brought over a mug of tea. 'Such a night,' he declared, his eyes shining brightly.

He sat down beside her, snow flecking his hair as it must have flecked her own. 'But it's all over now, Bridie,' he said happily. 'I can go back to my old house, and you can have your favourite room. The one you always have when you stay with me. We'll need to give everything a good scrub after the Crickbones, mind. But we'll pull through.' He gripped her hand tightly. 'The main thing is, we can go home.'

'But—' Bridie bit her lip, not wanting to dim the old man's happiness. How could she tell him the purpose of that night's adventure was not to win back his home, as he had taken it into his head to believe? How could it be? He had legally surrendered his yard—signed it away when he borrowed money from the Crickbones. Battle or no battle, he would remain homeless until the money was repaid. Every last penny of it.

Bridie was giving the matter serious thought when Miss Firbanks came across to her.

'Why so solemn, child?' she asked.

Bridie looked up studying the old woman's face. 'Miss Firbanks,' she said slowly, 'is it bad to do something you know is wrong to make another person happy?'

Miss Firbanks, thinking Bridie referred to that night, smiled. 'It depends how strongly you believe it important, child. Do you believe it important?'

Bridie nodded. 'Very.'

'Then you have your answer.'

Soon Miss Firbanks was called away to tend some of the street people hurt in the fighting and Mr Summers, despite himself, nodded off before the crackling fire. Bridie watched him contentedly sleeping. She leaned across and gently kissed him on the cheek. Then, making sure the blanket was drawn closely about him, she slipped away unseen.

The gates to Mr Summers's yard were wide open. Bridie crept in. The falling snow appeared brilliant in the darkness—white and sharply defined, whereas everything else was grey and indistinct.

At first she could not see the Crickbones—only hear them mournfully chanting to themselves.

'Big trouble . . . '

'Big trouble . . . '

'Big trouble . . . '

They sat upon the straw bales, two scarecrows tightly hanging on to each other. Snow upon their bowler hats. More comic than tragic.

'Big trouble . . . '

'Big trouble . . . '

'Big trouble . . . '

Swallowing the urge to say 'You've no one else to blame but yourselves', Bridie called out to them.

'Who is it?' hissed Amos suspiciously.

'Someone who's come as a . . . friend,' she said. 'I want to help you.'

'The Crickbones don't have no friends,' retorted Amos.

'And nobody helps them,' added Deakin poisonously.

Their voices melted into self pity. 'And when they try to help themselves all they do is land in big trouble . . . '

'Big trouble . . . '

'Big trouble . . . '

'Big trouble . . . '

'Are you in big trouble with Beau Scriven?' asked Bridie bluntly. 'Did he lend you money so you could get Gramps's yard? Is that how it was? And when you had Gramps's yard did he mean to use it for his cock fights while you lived at the house pretending it was just an ordinary business?'

'She knows!' shrieked Deakin.

'She's a spy,' said Amos darkly. 'Spies know everything.'

'Beau Scriven blames you for tonight, doesn't he?' pressed Bridie. 'Now the yard is no good to him he wants his money back.'

'Yes!' they screamed. 'Yes! Yes! Yes! And there's nothing left to give him!'

Bridie paused. 'I can help you . . . if you want me to,' she said slowly.

'How?' they sneered.

'By paying my grandfather's debt to you. That way you'll be able to give Scriven his money back. But—' she said firmly, 'once all scores are settled this yard must be returned to my grandfather.'

The brothers nodded furiously.

From around her neck Bridie pulled out a yellow ribbon. On the end was a key. She held it out to the Crickbones.

CHAPTER SIXTEEN

IT WAS SNOWING heavily when Bridie left the yard, flakes joining into misshapen clusters, falling through the air.

Glancing back at the opened gates she saw two pale faces watching her—two identical grins once again crooked with confidence. She shuddered and walked on, lowering her eyes in case she met the curry-paste Devil's mocking stare. She heard machinery grind and bellows wheeze and knew another smoke ring had appeared.

She reached Soap Hill without being missed. The fireside where she had left Gramps was deserted.

'We took him to our bus,' explained Selection Box, sidling up and giving her one of his wide brown grins. 'Poor old fella was worn out. Shivering in his sleep he was. It seemed cruel, dragging him all the way through the streets to the Bazaar.'

'Thanks, Selection Box,' smiled Bridie. 'You're a real friend. Do you think you and Spout Nose could take care of him for a couple more days? I have . . . things to do . . . before I can take him home.'

Selection Box saluted. 'A problem that is not,' he grinned.

'Ah, child, there you are,' called Miss Firbanks striding up, her coat now practically white with snow.

'Is something wrong?' asked Bridie guiltily.

'To be perfectly frank, child,' confided Miss Firbanks, her raucous voice not quite managing a whisper, 'it's my belief that the men have been drinking. Normally I wouldn't approve. But tonight is a victory and each man must celebrate in his own way. The trouble is, Branwell is unused to strong drink. I have warned him alcohol is a poison, yet he doesn't seem to pay the slightest heed.'

'But Spider—' uttered Bridie. 'How can Branwell be celebrating with Spider shot?'

Miss Firbanks clasped her hands (or she would have done if her sleeves weren't so long). 'That is the best part of all, child,' she declared. 'Spider is quite unharmed.'

'But I saw it happen,' insisted Bridie.

'You saw what you thought happened,' corrected Miss Firbanks. 'The truth is Spider's fur is so dense that the pellet simply lodged in it. I imagine it felt like a severe bee sting—enough to shock the poor creature quite senseless.'

'Well . . . that is something,' murmured Bridie.

Miss Firbanks peered sternly at her. 'What is the matter, child? You talk and act as if in a dream.'

Poor Miss Firbanks, thought Bridie sadly. I wish I could make you understand. But how can I when you think more of animals than you do of people?

Bridie made her excuses and left, drifting aimlessly between the fires. Faces there looked up at her, faces distorted by firelight and leery with drink, reminding her over and over of Amos and Deakin grinning like gargoyles. She turned quickly away, but heard the men freely passing bottles amongst themselves. Soon some were dancing drunk, stamping on the snow in boots done up with string, their whoops and shouts the only music.

Then she saw Branwell and stood watching him at a distance.

Despite the bitter cold, both his coat and shirt were open and sweat shone on his brow. He carried Spider as a small child might carry a toy, the unhappy creature bearing his discomfort with patience.

Suddenly Miss Firbanks rushed up ready to lecture him again.

'Mother!' he roared, his breath a whisky-reeking cloud. To her great surprise Miss Firbanks found herself hugged off the ground, her boots dangling in mid air, her hat knocked askew. 'We did it, mother!' he cried. 'We did it!'

He swigged from a bottle and thrust it on to Spout Nose.

'And that Beau Scriven better not show his face in these parts again,' added Spout Nose, squaring up his shoulders in readiness. 'We've shamed him into keeping away once and we'll do it again if needs be.'

Branwell snatched the bottle back before Spout Nose had had a chance to take a drink, and ignoring his friend's injured looks held it up until the firelight caught the smoothness of glass.

'Here's to you, mother!' he shouted. 'And to Bridie. And here's to the Byzantium Bazaar. May it go on for ever!'

Bridie turned away, hating herself more than anybody else in the whole world.

CHAPTER SEVENTEEN

THROUGHOUT THE NIGHT the snow fell thick and fast. The tyre fortress, the breakers' yard, and Soap Hill went under in snow.

Snow stopped the trains on the viaduct and snow ploughs quit the roads in defeat.

Then, towards the early hours, the dead weight of snow on the billboard's machinery made it strain and groan, whereupon the curry-paste Devil coughed out a cloud of petrol fumes and jammed, his mouth gaping in permanent surprise. Hell, it seemed, really had frozen over.

Around the Bazaar the wind sculpted drifts like white waves, breaking and remaking them, as restless as the tide.

Bridie lay awake listening to the wind moan. She rubbed her eyes. They felt hot and dry from lack of sleep. She rose, put on two more jumpers, a scarf, and a knitted hat and went shivering up the marble stairway.

Miss Firbanks looked up in surprise when she heard the door. She was not long risen herself. She was sitting on a bed brushing her hair.

She held out the brush to Bridie. 'Come, child,' she said. 'Make believe I am Shah.'

Without a word Bridie took the brush and set about the thick, greying hair. Miss Firbanks sat gazing at herself in a little silver hand mirror that was a companion piece to the brush. Occasionally she'd tilt it slightly to catch Bridie's pale reflection.

'You look worn out, child,' she observed.

Bridie shrugged. She was worried in case Miss Firbanks pressed her further, but suddenly the old woman flung aside the mirror and leapt up, carelessly scooping back her hair behind her ears. She had heard her cats and all else was forgotten.

Yet it was not the usual morning call that greeted them.

Miss Firbanks paused, listening, hairgrips in her mouth. On the stairway the steady mewl of hungry cats was fast breaking down into angry hisses and snarls.

'A fight?' she said, sounding and looking perplexed.

She hurried to the double doors and flung them open.

'Where is Shah?' Bridie heard her say. 'Why isn't he here conducting his duties . . . ? Shoo! you brutes . . . ! Get down there . . . ! Stop it I say . . . ! Bridie, here child! Quickly!'

Bridie went running out on to the landing. 'What is it, Miss Firbanks?'

The old woman was frowning. 'It's Shah—he isn't here.'

Peering over Miss Firbanks's shoulder, Bridie saw that the cats were like a boiling sea. They hissed like surf. Without Shah to maintain order they were irritable and fierce and beyond Miss Firbanks's control. Already several of the larger cats were nosing to the fore, determined to sit on the highest step. Chief among them were Pirate the black and white moggy and Buster the ginger tom; then came Caesar the half Siamese, the cross-eyed India, and Belladonna the great she-cat. Caesar's bleeding ear and the loose tufts of different coloured fur were evidence of earlier skirmishes.

The lesser cats supported each contender with claws and voices and even the lure of food failed to rally them.

'What on earth is going on?' demanded Branwell squinting up at the noise. He sounded as bad tempered as the cats.

'Shah's gone missing,' called Bridie.

Branwell shrugged. 'So? He'll be back when he gets hungry.'

'But, Branwell, you are missing the point,' said Miss Firbanks testily. 'Shah is always here—every morning without fail.'

Bridie tugged at Miss Firbanks's sleeve. The cats were now stirring and melting away, each one following its chosen leader, tails disdainfully risen like banners.

'I fear this is just the beginning,' said Miss Firbanks; and she was right; it marked the start of a tiresome day—of raids and battles and ambushes on every level of the Bazaar; and when the dust flew it truly flew, hanging in the air like brown smog.

Midday came grey and overcast with cloud, yet still with no sighting of Shah. High on the Bazaar's snowy parapets, cats sat posted like look-outs, gazing fixedly at the frozen city. They sat so still they might have been statues; and only when the wind made their fur eddy did they resemble the living creatures they really were.

As the afternoon wore on and the snow turned shadowy, Miss Firbanks grew as troubled as her cats. She climbed to the directors' room with a telescope, and every few minutes managed to find Bridie to ask, 'Have you seen him yet?'

Night was rapidly approaching. At every sound Miss Firbanks jumped and turned around. 'Could that be him, do you think? Could that be Shah?'

But it never was.

Branwell suggested they go out and search for him. It was not an entirely serious suggestion: after all, looking for a white cat in the snow even sounded a joke. But Miss Firbanks eagerly seized upon the idea.

'Yes—yes,' she muttered. 'It disturbs me to think of Shah outside on a night like this. I'll fetch my coat and hat.' She turned to Bridie. 'Child, will you help?'

Bridie found it difficult to speak. Her mouth was suddenly dry, her tongue not her own. 'S-sorry, Miss Firbanks . . . if you don't m-mind I would like to visit my grandfather.' It was a lie, and to her own ears an unconvincing one at that.

But it didn't seem to matter in any case. Miss Firbanks was hardly listening and Branwell was striding out of the door. Bridie felt so utterly miserable.

From the window in the directors' room, she stared out at the two small figures struggling to cross a grey field of snow. It was so cold she could taste it, and in between snow flurries she heard Miss Firbanks croaking out the name of her favourite cat.

Abruptly she tore herself away from the scene, finding that in a matter of minutes the room had become noticeably darker, the portraits on the walls black in dull frames. She shivered and cupped the candle close to her, for the moment needing its warmth more than its light.

It occurred to her this was the first time she had been alone at the Bazaar—not that she was afraid. Standing very still she listened to its half digested sounds, imagining she heard the air leaking out of each cavernous room, the rust flaking inside empty pipes, the stonework creak with cold, a joint settle like an arthritic bone . . .

So preoccupied was she by these imagined sounds that for a time she failed to notice the great noise put up by the dogs in the yard. When she did she frowned. Something must have disturbed them. Taking her candle she moved soundlessly to the top of the stairway.

'Miss Firbanks?' She breathed out the name. The candlelight flickered, rolling its light around the damp walls.

'Branwell?'

Really she knew it was neither of them, and for the first time felt apprehensive. She waited a moment before slowly going down, a step at a time, to investigate.

On the third landing she saw wet footprints glisten, and stopped, holding her candle low to study them. They were not the familiar worn prints of Miss Firbanks's wellingtons or Branwell's distinctive hiking boots. The tracks made a trail and ahead a door hung slightly open. Above it the sign said *Ladies Fashions*. From inside Bridie heard a sound, and approaching the door she nudged it. Slowly the door rolled back revealing a sight that filled her with curiosity and horror.

Before her the Crickbones were dancing, Deakin rocking back and forth on his great flat feet, his eyes closed and smiling in rapture. Amos had taken a mannequin from its stand and, holding it stiff and awkward in his arms, was waltzing the floor with it.

They kicked up so much dust that Bridie sneezed. The sound was as loud and unexpected as a gun shot.

At once the brothers stood still grinning at her, the mannequin at an angle, its wig hanging off.

Then, before Bridie could protest, Deakin seized her hand, and proceeded to dance her around and around as fast as he could.

'Where are they?' he whispered harshly into her ear. 'You told us they would be here. But there's nothing here but tatters for rag and bone men.'

'Not . . . here . . . ' gasped Bridie.

She was sent flying into Amos's arms and was forced to go twirling on with him.

'But you told us. You promised us they were here!'

He set her spinning like a top and she sank dizzy to the floor. When she looked up both brothers were coldly grinning at her.

'They're not here!' she cried. 'I'll take you to where they are. But before I do, have you brought the agreement you made with Gramps?'

A grubby piece of paper was dangled in front of her eyes. She glimpsed Mr Summers's signature and tried to snatch it.

'Ah-ah,' said Amos wagging a finger at her.

'You'll get what you want,' she said sullenly. She lunged at the piece of paper, grabbed it and tore it into shreds. She felt no happier for having done so.

'We have kept our word,' said Amos, his voice turning hard.

'Now keep yours,' added Deakin.

'Downstairs,' said Bridie. 'Not here, but downstairs.'

Chapter Eighteen

When bridie took the key on the yellow ribbon from Amos and unlocked the understairs door, the Crickbones glowered at her with deepest suspicion, as if suspecting a trap.

'They have to be stored down here,' explained Bridie in an exasperated tone. 'They need to be kept cool . . . Look, I'll go first if you don't trust me.'

'*I'll* go first,' snarled Amos.

'And *I'll* follow behind,' added Deakin.

So it was they went down the brick steps into the boiler room. Bridie showed them where the fur coats hung and was practically knocked aside by Deakin as he and Amos fell gloating upon them. Roughly the zippered bags were ripped open, the brothers sinking their bristly chins into the softness of fur, going snake-eyed in delight and slobbering with pleasure.

Bridie pulled her mouth tight.

'You best hurry up,' she said coldly. 'Miss Firbanks and Branwell will be back at any moment. Choose the four coats you want and get on your way.'

'Ah,' said Amos.

'Ah,' said Deakin.

With grins and knowing nods they glanced at each other, then turned to face Bridie.

'We have been thinking,' said Amos.

'And changing our minds,' added Deakin.

'We did agree four coats—y-e-s-s-s.'

'But we think we actually deserve more.'

'Well, I don't think you do,' cried Bridie.

104

'We'll take a vote on it,' suggested Amos.

'Those in favour—?' called Deakin.

The Crickbones lifted their hands in unison.

'Carried!' they declared.

They thrust out their chins, smug at their own deviousness.

Furious, yet unable to prevent them, Bridie could only watch as the brothers helped each other into a fur coat. They did so with much affected politeness. The coats swelled out their matchstick bodies and concealed their crookedness, but for all that both brothers still managed to resemble a seedy pair of second rate music hall comedians. Deakin sniffed at his sleeves as if mimicking the animal whose skin he now wore. Amos was taking many more coats off the rails and dumping them on the floor.

'But that's not fair!' protested Bridie. 'You have no right to do this . . . Put those coats back at once or I'll . . . I'll . . . '

Her threat trailed uselessly away as the Crickbones each took one of her hands and drew her up to the nearest half empty clothes rail.

'What—what are you doing?' she asked in a frightened whisper.

'We need you to help us,' said Amos.

'Did you think,' said Deakin, 'we could manage all on our own?'

Bridie felt the heaviness of a mink coat imprison her. It fell in thick folds to her feet, effectively preventing her from running away but, to make quite sure she did not even attempt to, Amos insisted on doing up every button himself.

'Mustn't catch your death,' he grinned and Deakin's grin was its mirror image.

Trapped like a fly in their web, Bridie soon found herself ushered outside in the snow. She felt utterly wretched as the Crickbones loaded up their old pram with stolen furs. It was very cold. Bridie turned up her collar, its touch soft against her cheeks. Stray flakes caught in its dark pile. Despite everything, she was glad of her coat.

The brothers closed the Bazaar's outer doors and came scuttling over, skeletons in ill-fitting skins.

'Best foot forward now,' smirked Amos.

'Heave-ho,' snickered Deakin.

'Oh, all right.' Bridie scowled at them and took up her place at the front of the pram which was the old-fashioned type, with big spoked wheels, and was heavy and awkward to manoeuvre through the snow. The wind blew in their faces, making the task much harder, but also covering up their tracks. Progress was slow.

'Don't just stand there, girl,' snarled Amos. 'Get your back into it.'

'She thinks she is a film star,' sneered Deakin. 'A film star in her mink coat.'

'Well, I think you look pretty stupid in yours,' retorted Bridie. 'Like . . . like . . . scrawny old bears!'

She bent down and pushed. The Crickbones pulled by the handle. More than once Bridie stood on her coat and tripped, falling face down in the snow.

Reaching the streets, they found the going less difficult. The Crickbones were wary, but the streets were quite deserted and traffic lights changed for traffic that didn't exist, so only a few people saw the peculiar little band go by; and absolutely no one witnessed it turn into Rivet Lane—except the curry-paste Devil, of course, and he was half blinded with icicles, his mouth still frozen open in disbelief.

Hot and exhausted they arrived outside Mr Summers's yard. Amos slyly glanced up and down the way and, seeing no one, unlocked the gate.

A mournful call greeted them.

'What was that?' asked Bridie. 'It sounded like a cat.'

Amos and Deakin caught each other's eye.

'Only the breeze, girl.'

'Or the hinges needing a spot of oil.'

'No, it wasn't,' cried Bridie. 'It was definitely a cat. And not just any cat. That was Shah!'

Slipping past the Crickbones and running as fast as the encumbering coat would allow, she burst into the snowy yard.

'Shah! Shah!' she called frantically.

She ran as if fighting to be free of the coat, its silky softness drowning her, the motion feeling less like running and more like swimming through fur.

The cat's pitiful wail arose again, answering her from behind the house. There she found Shah looking utterly bedraggled and with ice matting his fur. He was suspended from a window, in a metal cage too high up to reach. Bridie tried to jump, but only succeeded in jumping inside the coat, which never left the ground.

With the gates now securely locked behind them, Amos and Deakin could afford to take their time reaching her. When they did, Bridie rounded on them in a blazing fury.

'Why is Shah here?' she shouted.

Amos and Deakin stared coolly back, failing to comprehend her rage.

'It's the king cat,' said Amos.

'That Firbanks woman's favourite,' said Deakin.

'Like a witch . . . '

' . . . and her devil cat.'

'But what is he doing *here*?' demanded Bridie.

'We told you we would lure the Firbanks woman away . . . '

' . . . with that vicious son of hers.'

'We told you to wait and we would come and they would not be there.'

'We told you.'

'But I didn't think you were going to steal Shah. Miss Firbanks's been worried sick about him all day.'

'It's only a cat,' said Amos dismissively.

'Prowling vermin that eats other vermin,' said Deakin.

And together they said, 'We hate them all!'

They spoke with such vehemence that Bridie suddenly grew fearful for Shah. 'You will let him go?' she said hesitantly. 'You have what you want and more besides, so there's really no reason for keeping him any longer . . . '

The Crickbone brothers were busy unloading furs from the pram. They didn't pay her a scrap of attention. Bridie set her mouth firmly saying. 'All right, I'll release him myself,' although she didn't know how.

Deakin yanked the mink coat over her head, leaving her shivering in the cold.

'Perhaps we may soon skin a cat as easily,' he grinned.

'I'll see that you don't,' cried Bridie defiantly. 'I'm going to make sure Miss Firbanks knows. I shall tell her everything—even about the coats. And I don't care if I get into trouble. At least it'll stop you from hurting Shah!'

'We have locked the gates,' spoke the Crickbones together. 'You are going nowhere.'

Deakin said, 'Even so, brother, can we afford to take a chance while these coats are in our possession?'

Amos nodded thoughtfully. 'But when we no longer have them . . . '

' . . . when they are sold.'

'What proof will the girl have?'

'Didn't she say that, apart from the old woman at the Bazaar, she was the only one who knew of the coats' existence?'

'There will not be a shred of evidence against us.'

'Everyone will believe that *she* is the thief.'

'But until then—' grinned Amos.

'Until then—' Deakin grinned back.

Together they pounced upon Bridie, dragging her into the house.

CHAPTER NINETEEN

'LET ME GO! Get your hands off me! Leave me alone!'

Bridie became a wild thing. Biting, clawing, kicking, and lashing out with her arms.

The Crickbones withered before her, astonished and a little afraid. Perhaps they weren't expecting a young girl like her to fight back. Perhaps they thought she'd surrender meekly. If so, they were now learning by their mistake— and a painful lesson it was proving to be.

To their further dismay, the brothers found themselves hampered by their thick, bulky coats, and the silky, smooth fur that offered no grip. Every time they thought they had Bridie overcome, she simply slipped through their arms as if greased to swim the English Channel.

Landing Amos a smarting kick to his shin and smashing a sugar bowl at Deakin, Bridie took to her heels, escaping the kitchen and thundering up the stairs.

Smiling grimly the Crickbones stepped out of their coats and gave chase. They cornered her in Mr Summers's bedroom trying to barricade the door. They pinned her to the bed, both sitting on her to hold her down, and looking about as happy as if it were a rumbling volcano beneath them.

'What now?' gasped Deakin clutching his chest.

'Tie her up, of course,' answered Amos.

'Tie her?'

'Chain her.'

'Where—how?'

'I have a chain.'

'But where?'

Amos searched around with some urgency. 'The bed,' he concluded.

Deakin grinned. 'The bed,' he agreed.

Keeping a secure grip on her this time, they dragged Bridie to the foot of the bed and threw her down on the floor. The bed was made of brass tubing. The chain rattled. Bridie winced as it bit into her.

'Not such a wild cat now,' sneered Amos, making a great display of pocketing the key from the chain's padlock.

Deakin threw an old blanket into her face. She clawed it away and glared at him.

'Best you calm yourself down, girl, or none of us'll get any sleep.'

Bridie drew the back of her hand across her nose. 'What do you mean?' she asked.

Deakin's grin only widened and he clicked out the light. In the darkness Bridie heard heavy boots clump to the floor and the rustle of clothing. Then the bed rolled and groaned as the two brothers clambered in.

Deakin's voice said, 'On the whole, Amos, a successful day, I believe.'

'On the whole, Deakin,' agreed Amos. 'Goodnight, brother.'

'Goodnight, brother.'

The bed groaned again as the brothers worked themselves down under the blankets. Then it was still, and they smacked their lips, sniffed and sighed and began to snore, sometimes keeping perfect time with each other, sometimes one whistling in answer to the other's grunt.

Bridie shifted uncomfortably, her anger galling her more than the chain, which was only the final indignity. Outside she heard a small restless sound and remembered Shah cooped up in the cage. Without shelter he'd probably freeze by morning.

'And it will be my fault,' she told the darkness. 'If only I can get this chain off I might be able to do something.'

Gritting her teeth, she pulled until it hurt, vainly hoping to force a weak link. But although afterwards the chain bound her as firmly as ever, she had made a useful discovery. She found if she pulled hard enough it was possible to make the bed roll forwards on its castors, and this gave her the freedom to edge a little further along.

She pulled again—and once more the bed closed the gap on her. Soon she found it was easier if her arms did the pulling, not her middle; but she had to be more careful to keep the chain from rattling.

Bit by bit, edging forwards a few inches at a time, Bridie began to turn the bed towards the spot where Amos had carelessly thrown down his clothes.

The snoring continued uninterrupted, the movements too slight to disturb the sleeping Crickbones. Once Bridie glanced up and caught their faces squarely reflected in a dim dressing table mirror—mouths open, cheeks hollow. The sight made her sharply draw her breath and she waited a long time before attempting to move again, watching the brothers in their patched long johns, identical even in sleep. Then she tugged at the bed and it slid over the threadbare carpet, nudging painfully into her back.

At last her hard work and patience paid off. Reaching out, her hand touched something. Blindly she felt the collar and cuffs of a shirt before tossing it aside.

She reached out again and smiled as she reeled in Amos's trousers. Her hand went delving into a pocket and she winced when she realized she was touching a filthy handkerchief. A more useful find was the stub of pencil and piece of paper beneath it—both of which she kept.

Her heart was racing as she felt inside the other pocket. She pushed her hand in deep and . . . there it was; small and metal, her fingers closing tightly around it. Pulling out the key, it was all she could do to stop herself from cheering. A moment later the chain lay in a coil on the floor and she was free.

At the window the curtains were down—presumably as a result of the earlier struggle (although she couldn't precisely remember) and into the room stole an icy grey light. Without the benefit of a moon Bridie could see over the scrapyard as far as Soap Hill.

A flurry of snow stung the glass and there was a movement below the window ledge. It was Shah trying to turn away from the biting wind.

All at once he stared up at Bridie, his eyes dark and mysterious and with a power that made her want to shrink back into the shadows. Then he lowered his head, nuzzling the bars of his cage.

Bridie understood what he was telling her. 'Don't worry,' she whispered. 'I'll soon give you back your freedom . . . Then perhaps you will help me.'

By the snow light Bridie could see well enough to write a message. Taking the pencil and piece of paper she hastily scrawled: *HELP! Crickbones!!!—B*.

She wondered if it was too late to put matters right and if Miss Firbanks would ever forgive her. It was not a thought she cared to linger over.

The window opened without a sound. More worrying was the swirl of icy air that swept into the room. At once the snoring broke rhythm, Amos and Deakin smacking their lips and tasting the breeze. Bridie watched them, her breath stoppered up inside her. The Crickbones began to stir—pulling up the covers—on the very brink of waking; but then seemed to think better of it, turned and snuggled up to each other instead. Soon their snoring resumed, as regular as a saw rasping through a log.

Bridie let out her breath and quickly set to work.

The cage, she found, was suspended on a length of rope secured to a nail. It scraped against the wall as she hauled it up, Shah turning nervously inside. At last she pulled it into the room, setting it on the floor.

'Hush, Shah,' she whispered immediately. 'I know

you're glad to see me, but not a sound. Not a single purr.'

She lifted him from the cage and his gritty tongue touched her hand.

Taking her note, Bridie folded it and pushed it into his collar.

'Be sure not to lose it,' she pleaded. Holding up the great cat she kissed the top of his head. 'Now go, Shah. As fast as you can. Go find Miss Firbanks and let her know.'

Gently she dropped him through the opened window and he landed softly in the snow. He looked up, just once, then turned and bounded away, scudding over the whitened yard like a ghost.

Bridie carefully slid the window down and heard the Crickbones snoring. But luck had been with her so far— why not a little longer?

She crept past the bed. The door squeaked, the stairs creaked, each sound making her flinch as if at a pain. Finding one of the fur coats, she stepped out into the snow. There the cold air struck her, jolting her to her senses as if from a bad dream.

But she was growing too confident. She was not yet out of the yard, or safely back at the Bazaar. She thought these matters plain sailing, but had not counted on Shah having other ideas. High up on the car wrecks he began to call.

When Bridie heard him, her face fell. 'Oh no, Shah,' she implored. 'Please no.'

At first his call was weak, blown away by the wind. But gradually, as he found his voice, it cut across everything else.

It was only a matter of time before the cat-hating Crickbones heard him too. Sure enough, a few minutes later, a window flew open and Amos and Deakin appeared like Punch twice over in a Punch and Judy show. They sneezed violently at the cold. Bridie caught Amos's voice with its unpleasant tone. ' . . . And the devil cat has gone too—she has set it free to taunt us.'

'It is torture to our ears!' wailed Deakin.

'We should have killed it when we had the chance.'

'Yes. And that girl, she best watch her back too.'

The window crashed down almost hard enough to break its glass.

Shah meanwhile kept up his call as strongly as ever.

From the corner of her eye, Bridie caught the flicker of a shadow. Then another—and another. And, as she watched, she saw cats go streaming across the snow in answer to his summons. She recognized them as cats from the Byzantium Bazaar. Boswell . . . Gulliver . . . Sweet Pea . . . Pippen . . . and many more besides. But they did not turn to her or acknowledge her presence in any way.

When they had gone, Shah at last fell silent.

Then Bridie heard another sound—a door slam—and she knew the Crickbones were close behind.

CHAPTER TWENTY

SHE RAN TO the gates and found them impossibly locked. A quick glance at the lane-side fence revealed a different problem. Not its height—it was easily climbable, especially since the Crickbones had ruthlessly dumped all Mr Summers's stock against it (and an old railing, in such circumstances, is as useful as a ladder). No, it was the barbed wire along the top that posed the real problem.

Glancing behind, Bridie saw two shadowy figures and knew there was only one thing to be done. Slipping off her coat, she climbed up as near to the top of the fence as she could get and cast the coat over the barbed wire. The barbs looked viciously sharp and she hoped the fur would prove thick enough to do the trick.

There was only one way to find out.

She pulled herself up on to the coat and the coils of barbed wire immediately flattened beneath her. She slithered forward on her belly, feeling the wire bowing like metal ribs. Suddenly the wire sprang up again, tipping her off balance—sending her sliding head first into the lane outside. She screamed and instinctively threw out her arm, catching the coat by a sleeve. Her legs swung back under her and she jerked to a halt, dangling in mid air.

She hung there just long enough to hear the fur rip, then fell the last few feet into a deep snowdrift.

Tilting her head, she saw half the beautiful coat mangled on the barbed wire. She wrapped herself in the ragged piece that was left to her and ran stumbling through the snow. At the end of the lane she paused to look back. She might have guessed Amos and Deakin would not give up that easily. She saw them step out from the gates and turn on her with furious glares.

She pushed on. From somewhere a clock struck midnight, beating out twelve doleful chimes, which Bridie absently counted in her head. Thankfully it had stopped snowing, but the wind was getting up, blowing the settled snow like grit into her face and clothing—snaking before her in visible currents. On a roof, snow wrinkled, sliding to the ground with a muffled thud. But Bridie barely noticed.

Suddenly the snow became much deeper. All her strength and concentration were required to make any sort of progress at all; and in her wake the blizzard seemed to delight in creating shadows that might or might not be the Crickbones closing in. Cold and weary, she bowed her head, the ragged fur flapping loosely about her. She didn't notice the half hidden blink of warning lights until it was nearly too late. She pulled herself up just in time, standing on the very brink of a snow-covered hole.

Anger and frustration made her cry out—then she turned, startled, to a nearby doorway. From a cardboard box, set out of the wind, came a snuffling sound like an animal waking, and a voice from inside called, 'Oo is it? Oo's there?'

'Snail—oh, Snail!' cried Bridie, relief flooding through her body. She could have hugged the old woman when the familiar face blinked out at her.

''Ow d'you know m'name?' demanded Snail suspiciously. She didn't recognize Bridie, who was so encrusted in snow.

Bridie stumbled a few steps towards her, desperately trying to brush herself down. 'It's me, Snail—'

'Ahh . . . Miss Firbanks's girl.' Snail sniffed and the dew drop on the end of her nose gleamed. She didn't sound at all impressed.

'You must help me,' pleaded Bridie.

'Don't want no trouble,' muttered the old woman, her

head beginning to retract into her box like a turtle into its shell. 'Ain't seen nuffin'. Don't know nuffin'. Don't bovver no one.'

'Please, Snail!' cried Bridie. 'It's the Crickbones—they're right behind and if they catch me—oh, I don't know what they plan to do . . . Help me, Snail . . . Please . . . Help me . . . '

The wind blew, filling the silence between them.

'The Crickbones, eh?' Snail regarded the girl sternly, only the top half of her head visible, and only a patch of face between the box and balaclava at that. Bridie shivered and blinked the snow from her eyes; she must have made a pathetic sight. When she looked again she saw Snail emerge from her cardboard home, her old coat tied up with string and padded out with newspapers against the cold.

'Go, girl,' she said gruffly. 'You go to Miss Firbanks. Snail will slow up them Crickbones. An' you be sure t'tell Miss Firbanks jus' 'ow Snail 'as 'elped you.'

As she spoke, she began dragging at the protective barriers that surrounded the hole. Curiosity held Bridie longer than it should and kept her glancing back as she made her way up the street. She saw Snail skilfully reassemble the barriers right across the road and hang the warning lights upon them. Then, brushing down the sign (which was meant only for the pavement, and read: Danger—closed to pedestrians) she placed it in a prominent place. Now anyone coming by would mistakenly believe the entire road was closed. Last of all, Snail collected up the orange cones and, after giving each a brief polish with her elbow, lovingly placed them down at regular intervals like a grandmaster of chess setting out his pieces.

She chuckled as she put the last cone down, saying to herself, 'There. Let the city make o' this what it will when it wakes up in the mornin'.'

She was safely back inside her cardboard box when the Crickbones finally arrived.

'What does it say?' cried Amos pointing at the sign.

'D-an-ger,' read Deakin, screwing up his eyes.

'Danger?'

'Danger.'

'The girl has given us the slip.'

'She must have gone a different way.'

'What shall we do?'

'There is only one thing to do.'

'Go all the way round!'

They howled with rage.

'It does the temper no good at all,' muttered Amos darkly.

'Just wait till we get that girl,' growled Deakin.

Their voices were soon blown away by the wind. In her box Snail smiled to herself before drifting back to sleep and dreams of motorway roadworks.

Bridie fell to her knees in the shadow of the Bazaar, exhausted and half frozen, her fingers so numb she could hardly grip the key to turn it in the lock.

The bronze doors opened and she staggered in from the storm, stumbling blindly through the revolving doors, snow dropping from her in wet piles. After the brittle snow light, the darkness seemed dense and impenetrable; the silence unnerving following the blizzard's howl.

Finding Branwell's torch she clicked it on.

Shah did not flinch in its beam. He sat gazing directly back at her. Before him something lay white and crumpled on the floor.

Taking a few steps more, Bridie stared down at it. She recognized her note immediately, the big pasty writing looming up to accuse her. She *knew* then, there was no one there. Branwell and Miss Firbanks would have rushed to her aid the moment they read the note. They must have passed her on the way. And now she was all on her own at the Bazaar . . . Well, not quite . . .

Something pushed hard against her legs and she nearly stumbled. Shah was rubbing himself against her, his purrs vibrating the air.

CHAPTER TWENTY-ONE

SHAH WOULD NOT leave Bridie's side—not for a moment—bounding up the stairway after her, as she went in search of dry clothing.

At first Bridie was so cold and shivery she failed to notice his affectionate rubs and nuzzles for what they were.

'Go away, Shah,' she said, angrily shoving him aside. 'Stop getting under my feet.'

But Shah was determined to be noticed. He stalked the trailing leg of her jeans, pouncing on it as if it were a mouse; then made a nest in the clothes Bridie brought out for herself, kneading the jumpers with his claws—until growing bored with that, he knocked the whole lot on to the floor. Bridie didn't notice. She was furiously scowling at herself in a flaking mirror, trying to make her numbed fingers obey her. She nearly wept over the effort it required just to put on a pair of jeans, then managed to get into a hopeless tangle with her sleeves. As for buttons and laces . . . the less said about them the better.

Shah crossed his paws and watched with what might have passed for wry amusement in the cat world.

At last Bridie pulled her head through a jumper. 'Well?' she asked. 'Do you think I look more human now?'

Shah turned his lazy eye upon her as if to say that was her concern, besides what was so marvellous about looking human?

Bending down, Bridie stroked his head and the cat raised himself to her hand. 'What's going to happen next, Shah?' she whispered. Shah purred and Bridie, growing more thoughtful said, 'Whatever it is, one thing's for sure, I'm going to have to be honest with Miss Firbanks. I owe her that at least.'

She decided to go downstairs and wait for Miss Firbanks's and Branwell's return, and confess everything the minute they came through the door. After that . . . well, Miss Firbanks must decide for herself . . .

Shah rubbed against her heels as he followed her back down.

By the light of one small candle Bridie sat on a stool writing her name over and over in the dust on the counter before her—that was until Shah jumped up on to her lap, demanding her fullest attention.

Bridie laughed. 'But you're Miss Firbanks's cat,' she teased. 'Ow, Shah! Stop it—you're hurting!'

Shah suddenly dug his claws into her and stared at the main entrance. Bridie followed his gaze. She saw the revolving doors slowly turn, whereupon all the words she had been carefully rehearsing vanished from her head.

Her nervousness increased when two torches clicked on. She hurried towards them, even though, at the back of her mind, a small suspicion grew that something was not right or as it should be. The torch beams swept the darkness as if one—like *twin* beams. The phrase brought her up sharp along with a terrible idea. What if the Crickbones had made a copy of the master key while it was in their possession? Such a key would prove invaluable, now they knew where to find the coats—they could come and go at will, helping themselves to as many more as their greed permitted.

She stopped walking, but it was too late for caution. The two beams shone straight into her face.

She threw up a hand to shade her eyes. 'Why have you come?' she asked fiercely.

A long pause followed before Amos spoke.

'You ruined one of our coats,' he said accusingly.

'That means we're owed another,' said Deakin.

'You can put it on when we take you back with us.'

The torchlight jerked as they made a sudden lunge for her—but Bridie was wary of their treachery and dashed towards the marble stairway.

'Stop her! Stop her!' the Crickbones were howling, scuttling after her like enraged spiders.

In the darkness, Bridie had to be sure of her footing. Reaching the first floor landing, she flung herself through the double doors of the furnishing department, slamming them so hard after her that dust trickled from the ceiling on to the dark, cobwebby shapes of chests, chairs, and cabinets. With a moment's calm reflection she knew if she could only stall the Crickbones for long enough, chances were that Miss Firbanks and Branwell would return. She cast round for a suitable place to hide.

Seeing the table she dived underneath it. Not a second too soon. At that instant the doors re-opened and the beams of two torches probed the darkness like an insect's antennae.

'Girl?' called Amos.

'Oh, girl!' called Deakin.

'Gir-lie!' they called together. 'Have no fear, we shall find y-ou!'

'And when we do,' snarled Amos, 'you will wish we hadn't.'

The light flashed Bridie's way again—and to her horror she glimpsed her footprints in the dust making a trail that led straight to her hiding place. How could she be so stupid not to realize?

'We know where you are, girl,' rose Amos's confident voice, much closer now than before. Bridie panicked and, bolting from beneath the table, ran straight into his waiting arms.

CHAPTER TWENTY-TWO

TOO WEARY TO resist, Bridie put all her efforts into shouting at the top of her voice for someone to come—and yet Amos and Deakin made no attempt to quieten her. Indeed they merely laughed.

'Make as much noise as you want, girl,' taunted Amos.

'See who it brings,' said Deakin. 'We'll tell you who—'

'Nobody!'

They grinned smugly.

'We saw 'em.'

'The Firbanks woman, that son of hers, and his ape creature.'

'We saw 'em in the snow. Going away.'

'They didn't see us.'

'But we know they're not here . . . '

'Only you and us here . . . '

Deakin's face slid greasily into a snigger, Amos's face twisted into a leer; and between them was Bridie who knew they were speaking the truth. But determination as much as fear made her continue shouting as loudly as ever.

'Miss Fir-banks! Bran-well!'

Then she violently recoiled from the Crickbones. Despite what they had said, they were now trying to silence her, clamping their hands over her mouth, and Bridie sensed panic in their urgency. Did this mean someone *had* come after all? The expression on the brothers' faces was scowling as they scanned the shadowy department.

'Miss F—' Joyously Bridie struggled to make herself heard through the stifling fingers.

'Shut up, you little fool!' she heard Deakin breathe. 'We

123

told you she ain't here. It's *them* that have come. *Them*.' His voice trembled trying to find the appropriate words. 'Them screechers—them hell creatures! Them *cats*!'

Only now after he had spoken was Bridie aware of a general movement all around—a stirring amongst the old armchairs, a gathering of numbers on the other pieces of furniture. In the Crickbones' torchlight, eyes gleamed, staring back with a steadiness of purpose.

The Crickbones' terror further increased when a great white cat leapt noiselessly on to a pedestal table nearby and without a touch of malice sat casually licking his paws. Shah, of course, and Bridie felt the Crickbones' bodies tighten into knots.

Suddenly Deakin clutched his throat, his breathing a mixture of hollow wheezes and wet splutters, and his eyes bulging.

'Can't brea-the! Can't brea-the!' He was turning scarlet.

Amos was turning scarlet too, but for an entirely different reason. He was gripped by fury.

'Call 'em off!' he commanded. 'Call 'em off now!'

'How?' asked Bridie. 'They aren't dogs . . . Besides these are Miss Firbanks's cats, not mine.'

Slowly, with lowered heads, the cats pressed forwards. They moved as if by a pre-arranged signal, those high up dropping softly to the ground; with every eye fixed on the Crickbones themselves. Only Shah remained aloof, sitting on the table carefully and thoroughly grooming himself as if he had no other care in the world.

Finally Deakin could bear it no longer. With a scream he leapt into a wardrobe, slamming the mirrored door after him. The cats momentarily caught their own reflections— before the entire wardrobe tipped back from the impact of Deakin's weight . . . wavered uncertainly . . . lost balance and, with a gathering momentum, went toppling over.

Deakin screamed wildly from inside, thinking the cats somehow to blame.

But this was merely the beginning. Deakin's wardrobe hit another, knocking it hard into a third which fell against a fourth . . . until a whole line of wardrobes was crashing down like dominoes. The noise was incredible. Amos's nerve broke. Pushing Bridie aside, he bolted through the ranks of cats and fled up the marble staircase.

Shah dropped off the table at the same instant and bounded after him, drawing every other cat with him too.

Last of all followed Bridie—but not before turning the key in the wardrobe's lock to prevent Deakin escaping. He hammered furiously to be let out.

Bridie felt dizzy at the turn around in events. By the time she was out on the landing, she could see Amos's torchlight much higher up, and hear his boots clumping on the stairs. Of the cats, there was nothing either to see or hear, but she knew they were still in pursuit, tormenting Amos by their very presence.

Without knowing why, Bridie had an awful sense of something terrible about to happen. She leapt up the stairs two, sometimes three, at a time calling, 'Wait, Amos! The cats won't hurt you. Just wait for me!'

She heard him cough and splutter as Deakin had done.

Reaching the top landing, he turned and aimed a vicious kick at Shah, who leapt back, spine arched and spitting.

Only one door presented itself to him now—the self-important mahogany door to the directors' room. Amos burst in and his shriek of rage came almost at once. He reappeared, backing away, followed by a crush of quizzical, mewing cats.

'Keep them off me!' he begged, first pressing himself against the banister, and then inching himself up on to it. Innocently the cats sat gazing up at him, their numbers growing all the time, their voices joined in a discordant wailing.

'Amos! Be careful!' shouted Bridie, hovering uneasily on the stairway just below him.

She saw him waver, his arms outstretched like a bird about to fly and his light shining upwards at the cobweb-vaulted ceiling.

Then slowly he fell backwards, dropping down the stairwell—his scream seeming to go on and on for ever—until with a sickening abruptness it ended.

Silence.

Bridie sank down upon the cold steps, her own horrified scream still ringing in her head. In the darkness she didn't dare move, and clung to the banisters in case she too went spiralling away as Amos had done. Around her, cats yawned, lazily stretched and quietly dispersed to their various nightly haunts about the Bazaar. In that single moment Bridie hated them all, and most of all she hated Shah.

She remained there alone, desperately clinging on as if to some life-raft until Miss Firbanks and Branwell returned.

Seeing their light gradually creep up the stairs, she ran down and threw herself against Branwell, burying her face into Spider's fur.

Miss Firbanks held up her hurricane lamp. 'Heavens, child,' she said briskly. 'What on earth has been going on?'

'Y-you didn't see h-him?' sobbed Bridie. 'You didn't s-see him at the f-foot of the stairs?'

'Whom, child?' asked Miss Firbanks firmly. 'You are not making a scrap of sense at the moment.'

'Amos of course! He's d-dead. He must b-be. He fell from h-here.'

'Amos?' Miss Firbanks and Branwell looked at each other mystified. 'But there's no one there, child,' said Miss Firbanks softening her tone. 'No one at all.'

'But there must be!' insisted Bridie. Then she remembered Deakin.

'Where are you going now?' called Miss Firbanks, as Bridie pushed past them and clattered down the stairs.

In the furnishing department only the lightest dust still hung hazy in the air. Bridie picked up Deakin's fallen torch. Cat prints lay everywhere and the wardrobes leaned together like bar-room drunks.

In the mirrored door of the first wardrobe Bridie took a long hard look at herself before turning the key to unlock it. The wardrobe was empty. She stepped inside beating its walls like a magician with his magic box.

'The back's off,' she shouted to Miss Firbanks and Branwell, who stood anxiously watching at the doorway. 'Deakin's kicked the plywood back off and got away.'

Miss Firbanks came across, took her arm and guided her to a dusty sofa, making her sit down beside her.

'You are still gabbling, child,' she said. 'Now, suppose you give a full account of what happened here tonight.'

So Bridie told her. It wasn't easy and she left nothing out in order to present herself in a better light. For the most part Miss Firbanks sat very still, frowning as she listened. Only once did she speak and then with great passion.

'Those evil coats!' she cried out. 'I told you they were cursed and this has but proved me right!'

Afterwards she questioned the girl closely and, of course, Branwell was curious to learn more, since he wasn't aware of the coats' existence in the first place.

Miss Firbanks shook her head sadly. 'Poor, wretched Deakin. He will be lost without his brother.'

'Do you think he has taken Amos's body with him?' asked Bridie.

'I shouldn't doubt it,' said Miss Firbanks matter of factly.

'This is a bad business all round,' said Branwell. 'Shouldn't we at least notify the police?'

Miss Firbanks waved her hand, dismissing the idea. 'No,' she said. 'Let Deakin alone to his grief a while.'

'But we must do something,' insisted Branwell.

'I suggest we all go to bed,' replied Miss Firbanks, rising to her feet. 'This day has been overly eventful and far too distressing. I for one shall be grateful when it has reached an end.'

She turned to leave.

'Miss Firbanks . . . ' said Bridie in a low, timid voice. The old woman stared at her. 'I'm . . . sorry.'

'You, child?' said Miss Firbanks astonished. 'What have you to reproach yourself with? This is entirely my fault. I should have rid myself of these coats while I had the chance. Then perhaps this terrible business would never have happened.'

CHAPTER TWENTY-THREE

WITHOUT FRIENDS OR relations, there was no one in the city to care about the Crickbones—the tragic death of Amos, and Deakin's sudden disappearance. And although Bridie kept a careful watch on the local newspapers, the daily headlines remained preoccupied by the great freeze. Once she saw a photograph of the curry-paste Devil, his chin bearded with icicles: underneath the caption read: *Cold continues—Thaw on the way.*

Mr Summers could do nothing about his yard with the snow so thick on the ground, but with Bridie's help, he set about scrubbing his house from top to bottom, eliminating all trace of the Crickbones from every room, until it was as if they had never been there in the first place.

Branwell, however, warned they must remain wary of Deakin. When Mr Summers enquired why, Branwell looked serious.

'He may hold Bridie responsible for his brother's death,' he said; and he helped change the locks on the gates and doors. They turned remarkably smoothly, considering the years they had languished in the Bazaar's hardware department.

Of course Bridie tried to spend as much of her remaining time as possible at the Bazaar. The animals still needed looking after, and Miss Firbanks hadn't realized quite how much she'd come to depend upon the girl, so was always glad to see her, raucously shouting out some command or other the moment she appeared and expecting Bridie to fall instantly into step like a soldier.

One afternoon Miss Firbanks told Bridie she had a

special task for her, and Bridie felt uneasy when she led the way to the understairs door. The boiler room lay undisturbed and despite the briefness of her previous two visits, Bridie's memories were vivid enough to raise goosepimples.

'Help me, child,' called Miss Firbanks, sweeping an armful of coats off a rail, against the coat-hangers' jangled protests.

The coats were dragged upstairs into the courtyard at the back of the building. In their pens the dogs watched as the heap grew steadily larger. It was all but complete when Branwell appeared, holding Spider in his arms, and accompanied by Mr Summers who was leading Trotter.

Miss Firbanks thoroughly doused the coats with a can of paraffin.

'Your matches if you please, Branwell,' she said holding out her hand.

A single match was struck. It flamed bright yellow. Miss Firbanks held it a moment, considering, then simply let it drop. The pile instantaneously combusted, snatching an angry gulp of air.

With the flames came smoke and a powerful smell. The dogs barked at the vague animalness of it, and Spider covered his nose with his paws. Nobody spoke, understanding this to be a solemn moment, as the blue flames climbed higher and higher.

Secretly, from the shadows, there was another who watched too.

It was Deakin.

He had about him the look of a half starved stray. He was even more dirty and unkempt than usual, and the stubble on his chin had grown into a beard. Only his eyes retained their former wily spark. Hungrily he observed the scene as such an animal would observe fresh meat, and a cold, sinister grin appeared.

He was upon them before they knew it, seizing Bridie

and dragging her to the very edge of the fire. 'Stay where you are!' he shouted at the others. 'Or I'll ... I'll ... '

His expression sagged with misery. '*I*,' he said brokenly. 'Meaningless little word ... *I* ... One letter, you see ... One ... Alone ... By itself and friendless ... *We* and *us* need two letters. Two! Like brothers—together!'

He glowered across at Branwell who was trying to edge round to reach him and the poison inside him boiled up once more. 'Take another step,' he hissed, 'and it shall go bad for the girl ... Yes ... It shall be as the good book teaches ... An *I* for an *I* ... ' He glanced round expectantly for someone to finish his sentence, as once someone would have done, and again was utterly dejected.

'A-mos!' he howled. 'Why did you leave me here like wicked Abel who left Cain; and though the clouds turned black and stormy, the animals still went into the Ark two by two. I would never have left *you*, Amos. Not standing alone in the rain. Not alone!' He glared at Bridie in a way that frightened her more than the flames leaping up at her feet. 'And all because of *this* girl,' he said with real menace. 'All because of *her*.'

Miss Firbanks held out a hand to him. 'Listen to me, Deakin,' she said firmly. 'Is this fair to the memory of Amos—think of your poor dead brother.'

Deakin sneered at her, his crooked face suddenly as cocksure as it used to be. 'Amos ain't dead. I won't let him die.' He clutched at his chest. 'I keep him alive inside me. Here. In our heart. We cannot be closer. See—see. We share the same shadow and breathe the same air.' He slyly lowered his head beside Bridie's. 'And we desire the same revenge.'

A malicious smile crept across his face, and despite the fire's intense heat, Bridie felt numb with cold, shivering violently and unable to cry out. The flames stirred, seeming to reach out for her.

Then she heard Miss Firbanks speak.

'What nonsense you spout, Deakin,' said the old woman briskly. 'Why all this talk about revenge if, as you say, Amos is alive. Unless,' she added shrewdly, 'he really is dead after all.'

Bridie saw Deakin wince at the dilemma this posed him. He jerked her against his bony rib-cage. 'Amos is alive. Amos is alive,' he gabbled as if to convince himself.

'Then let the girl go,' said Miss Firbanks softly.

Deakin let out a disgusted hiss and, shoving Bridie to the ground, wolfishly eyed the fire, determined to salvage something now that he was cheated of his revenge. Seeing a coat at the fire's edge, he grinned lopsidedly then plucked it from the flames. It was singed and smoking, but not yet alight. Holding it high above his head, he called, 'We will take this coat to keep us warm. A travelling coat to wear when we go away and leave this hateful place for ever.'

He ran laughing through the open gateway, flying the coat after him.

'Stop him!' cried Branwell, but Miss Firbanks caught his arm.

'Let him go,' she said. 'It is of no great consequence.'

She cast a dispassionate eye at Bridie, who was trying to reassure her fretting grandfather as he brushed her down, breaking off to cup her face in his hands.

'Are you all right, child?' she called.

Bridie nodded and Miss Firbanks said no more on the matter, crossing instead to the fire.

'Look at the flames,' she said, excitedly hugging her arms to her. 'See how well the coats burn . . . ' She turned to Bridie. 'I had hoped this might be somehow special, child. The lifting of the curse. But it seems the curse has spread its final shadow over us—still I will try my best to make amends.'

So saying she left the fire and marched off into the Bazaar.

'What does she mean?' Bridie asked Branwell.

He shrugged, as mystified as she was.

'Look,' said Mr Summers. 'Here comes Miss Firbanks again—carrying a silver platter. Has she prepared a feast for us?'

He rubbed his hands in anticipation, but Bridie could only dredge up the memory of that awful cloying grey stuff that was Miss Firbanks's usual fare; and glancing at Branwell, saw the same look of foreboding as one who had also tasted it.

'Well, come along,' called Miss Firbanks briskly. And when they were gathered around her, she lifted the silver serving lid with a triumphant flourish, revealing an array of . . . cakes. Vanilla slices, éclairs, little round cheesecakes, cherry tarts, and florentines.

Branwell and Bridie stood staring at her open-mouthed in amazement, until Miss Firbanks became flustered with embarrassment. 'It was a whim,' she said wringing her hands. 'Purely a whim. I just happened to be passing the shop and I saw them and I went in. I know it was too, too extravagant of me. Such exorbitant prices for a few sugary confections. But I bought them and brought them home and, well, here they are . . . ' And when their incredulous eyes still did not lift from her, she blurted out, 'I wanted it to be a celebration—and this is the sort of frivolity people indulge in at parties!'

Mr Summers, unencumbered by old prejudices, had already helped himself to an éclair. He bit straight into it, cream spurting out and down his chin, spotting his waistcoat and splodging on to the ground, where Spider was waiting. Dipping in his paws Spider elegantly licked his tiny brown fingers one at a time. Bridie laughed to see him, so did Branwell. Miss Firbanks smiled awkwardly.

Then they all helped themselves to a cake—even Miss Firbanks, who turned giggly, lolling her head from side to side, as if it were possible to become intoxicated on sugar-icing—and in her case she probably thought she could.

The fire was dead and the cakes all eaten when Bridie and her grandfather said their goodbyes and left, Mr Summers leading Trotter, with Bridie riding upon his back. The snow was all but melted, lasting only in dirty piles scattered here and there. High above, dark clouds rolled by, yet the light was clear, as the city stood on the verge of spring, with even the drabbest building revealing new colours in readiness— be it the delicate pink of a brick wall or the blue-grey of a slate roof; and in the distance a limestone steeple shone, caught in a single shaft of pale light.

The city is waking from its hibernation, thought Bridie; and only the broken-down curry-paste Devil carried the winter's shabbiness with him. Turning into Rivet Lane, Bridie felt confident enough to meet him full in the eye again—but no longer cared to do so. She fixed her gaze on the silver wisps curling over her grandfather's collar, knowing there was something she must ask.

'Gramps.'

'Hmm?' The old man didn't turn around.

Bridie frowned to herself. 'I suppose,' she said hesitantly, 'I'll have to go back to Aunt Dolly's soon . . . That is, when she gets completely better.'

'I suppose you will,' mused Mr Summers. 'Why? . . . Don't you want to?'

'No,' cried Bridie passionately. 'Oh, Gramps, it isn't that I'm ungrateful to her or anything like that, it's just that I want to stay here with you and Miss Firbanks and Branwell.'

They walked a little further in silence, Mr Summers waiting his moment. It seemed there was something *he* needed to tell Bridie.

'Had a letter come this morning,' he announced casually. 'From your Aunt Dolly it was.'

'Oh.' Bridie was surprised he hadn't mentioned it earlier.

'Appears your aunt is getting married.'

'*Married!*' exclaimed Bridie.

The long and the short of it was, that while she was in hospital Aunt Dolly had received a daily visit from one of her regular *paying guests*, as she called them, a certain Mr Rogers. At first he brought her grapes (seedless because they are tidier to eat), then flowers (daringly real ones at that) and then a proposal which she had accepted, and all the nurses had burst out in applause. She would still need a lot of caring for, even after she left hospital and, well, it was safe to assume Bridie's stay at Gramps's would be considerably longer than was originally intended.

'But that's wonderful news,' cried Bridie and she laughed at a sudden thought. 'I don't know how Aunt Dolly will take to being called Mrs Dolly Rogers. With a name like that, she ought to be a pirate!'

Mr Summers chuckled as he unlocked the gates to his yard. From their pens, the cockerels he had rescued from the wreckers' yard came out to peer at them.

'Why didn't you tell me this, this morning,' asked Bridie, 'when the letter first arrived?'

Mr Summers shrugged. 'To tell you the truth, Bridie, I didn't know if you'd be pleased or not. Perhaps I thought you wouldn't care to stay here with a foolish old man like me.'

Bridie slid off Trotter's back and by way of an answer gave her grandfather a hug.

'Why, it's Tom,' she heard him say.

She turned around and to her delight saw Shah watching them.

She called him and the great white cat jumped up into her arms. Curiously she said, 'Why did you call him Tom, Gramps?'

'Because that's his name. He's my old king cat, who left when the Crickbones came. I guess he must have gone to Miss Firbanks's and made himself boss there.'

'Well, I shall never call you Tom,' said Bridie fussing him. 'To me you'll always be Shah of the Byzantium Bazaar. It sounds much grander than plain old Tom of Summers's Yard.'

Then Shah leapt down and disappeared for a moment. When he returned he was carrying something heavy in his mouth. At first Bridie thought it was a mouse. A present like those received by Miss Firbanks each morning.

Gently he placed the object at Bridie's feet.

It was a silver hairbrush.

Other books by Stephen Elboz

The House of Rats
ISBN 0 19 271664 6

Winner of the 1992 Smarties Young Judges Prize for the 9–11 age category.

One damp foggy morning, the man who called himself the master threw down his napkin and strode out from the great house, never to return.

Esther, Zachary, Carl and Frankie are happy, living in the mysterious great house, until suddenly the master vanishes and everything changes. The safe routines disappear. The wolves which roam the forest outside, howling for food, become a real threat; while inside the house, other people start to take over their lives.

Without realizing it, the children are in great danger. But then, just when they think there can be no escape, they meet one of the 'Rats'. And they begin to discover the secrets of the amazing house.

'I loved the vividly realised characters, the warmth and wit of *The House of Rats*. This is a fine novel.'
Times Educational Supplement

'A brilliant story which grips you from the first to last page.'
Mail on Sunday

The Games-Board Map
ISBN 0 19 271701 4

Beware of snakes, especially the slippery-backed varieties which are most treacherous of all.

When Hebe begins the games-board adventure, it takes her a while to realize what is going on. But soon she has to believe that the impossible is happening all around her. From the musical chairs (who sing, of course), to bats and pirates, it's a crowded world. Hebe has to share the games board with all kinds of creatures: the bishop from the chess game who complains about 'those confounded draughts'; various pawns (or prawns?), and probably snakes too—after all, there are ladders.

What Hebe really wants to do is to get home, eventually. But it's not as easy as all that . . .

'A most unusual, original and inventive book.'
Children's Books of the Year

Bottle Boy
ISBN 0 19 271718 9

Treasure isn't always gold and silver, as Mouse discovers. There's a fortune to be made from old glass bottles if only you know where to look . . .

Mouse escapes from a life of crime and hardship, and sets off to find his treasure. But instead he finds a whole lot of new troubles. There's the Pendred Gang, who instantly become his sworn enemy; the strange old man with a shotgun; the everyday struggle just to survive. And it's not long before Mouse's past catches up with him, secrets are revealed, and the real danger begins.

'A superb thriller for nine- to 12-year-olds.'
Sunday Telegraph

'This is Stephen Elboz' third novel which will add to his reputation as a stimulating writer for children.'
Junior Bookshelf